# The quarterback paused in calling the signals

He looked over to his coach and then in the direction of the man's outstretched arm.

The bony finger was pointed at Carl Lyons.

The quarterback nodded slowly, a grinning skull rocking inside a large helmet, and resumed calling the play.

"Down! Set! Fifty-two! Ironman! Ironman! Hut! Hut!"

The line exploded into action, and then it was Lyons alone against the other team. Only there was no ball, no first down—just eleven men coming to kill him.

He scrabbled for the Uzi and emptied it at the rushing mass. Some went down, but others kept coming. When the machine gun locked open and empty, he grabbed for the .45.

It wasn't there.

With a curse, he discarded the Uzi and turned to meet the onslaught. The Ironman had nothing left to fight with but his body and his guts.

**Mack Bolan's**

# ABLE TEAM

# CAJUN ANGEL

**Dick Stivers**

A GOLD EAGLE BOOK FROM

# W RLDWIDE

TORONTO • NEW YORK • LONDON • PARIS
AMSTERDAM • STOCKHOLM • HAMBURG
ATHENS • MILAN • TOKYO • SYDNEY

For Gene,
In memory of Karen

First edition December 1986

ISBN 0-373-61227-3

Special thanks and acknowledgment to
Chuck Rogers for his contributions to this work.

Printed in Canada

# PROLOGUE

*El sitio de los féretros de los muertos.*

Translated literally, the phrase meant "the site of the coffins of the dead." It was the closest thing this godforsaken place had to a morgue or a mortuary.

The blond man grimly steeled himself for what he knew lay ahead.

He was in Mexicali, a moderate-sized city on the Mexican side of the international border, just inland from Tijuana.

The shabby building crowded the street. Most of the paint—originally a nauseating mustard color—had flaked off. The old stucco, long past its prime, had fallen from the walls in irregular patches. The resulting surface consisted of leprous splotches connected by cracks that straggled across the walls like meandering vines.

Sewer smells lay over the entire area like a dirty blanket. The stench permeated the buildings and the noisy, narrow streets.

"Jesus," muttered the man, "what a fucking garbage dump to be dead in."

On the other hand, he thought belatedly, an instant after you're dead, it doesn't matter anymore.

He hoped not, anyway.

A trio of dark youths lounged against the wall of the morgue, thin faces beneath greasy black hair.

They fell silent as the stranger approached. Moments after he had passed one of them made a remark in Spanish. The other two laughed loudly. The lewdness in their laughter coupled with their proximity to the *sitio de los féretros*, suggested that the remark had something to do with necrophilia and the rugged, blond *norteamericano*.

If they had looked more closely, the youths might have thought again about the remark and their laughter.

They would have seen that the gringo was six feet tall, give or take a fraction. Any of them with an eye for weight would have put him around two hundred pounds, none of it fat.

He didn't look like a bodybuilder exactly, though his arms and shoulders were heavily muscled. The deltoids were thick, the back tapering in a powerful V from shoulders to waist. Cordlike veins ran up the muscular forearms and disappeared beneath the knit shirt that covered the man's upper arms. A single vein the size of a soda straw lay along the outer surface of the biceps and stood out in sharp relief beneath the shirt.

In a word, he looked rugged. Buffed out. Tough. Not somebody to mess with, even for three knife-carrying *pachucos*.

Moreover, if any of the punks had been exceptionally perceptive, they would have seen something else as well. Something that would have made them hold their tongues even more than the man's physique had.

It had to do with the eyes.

Taking a glacier and adding a little more blue would give about the right effect. Hard. Cold. Icy. But there was more to it than just their color. Somehow, it was the life in them. *Bleak* would describe it. There was a certain flintlike grimness to them, something that said that these eyes had perhaps seen too many places and too much of life that wasn't good.

"Tired eyes," a woman had once called them as she touched the creases that framed their corners.

The eyes of a killer.

At the sound of the laughter, the blond man stopped in his tracks.

He had understood the unwholesome implication of the young man's remark even though his ability to speak Spanish was limited. For a moment, he was tempted to wheel on the young men, snatch them right out of their U.S.-made tennis shoes and counsel them concerning their demeanor.

He was good at that kind of "counseling."

The blond man had spent several years with the Los Angeles Police Department, working the worst streets in a city that has a lot to offer in the way of bad streets. He had rapidly earned the reputation of being tough but fair, and utterly fearless. Compared to the work he had done since then—work that made him one of a handful of the most dangerous men in the world— L.A.'s mean streets were Club Med.

It wasn't fear that stopped him now.

The punks were nothing. The fact that he would automatically be presumed guilty by the authorities and could well end up in a Mexican jail was something more to think about but not even that really worried him.

No, it was something else entirely. Smart-ass punk bullshit was a minor annoyance compared to his reason for being there.

If his information was correct, a lovely woman was dead.

And, the man reflected, his information probably *was* correct—the source of the news, a place known to a select few as Stony Man Farm, rarely made mistakes.

He was there to confirm or deny it, to make the identification. It was a mission of sorts, a mission of death.

Moreover, it the body turned out to be who they thought it was, there could be little doubt but that she was dead because of him. In a way, he would have killed her. Not directly, but by who he was, by what he did. He would undoubtedly have caused her death.

Still standing motionless, the blond man thought of the woman whose body he might soon be seeing in this squalid dump. She had been a gentle, idealistic lady with brown hair and slim legs and a firm conviction that there was no such thing as a bad boy. She'd been his first love years ago when he was a rookie cop, driving a patrol car around for the LAPD. But things hadn't worked out back then, and their roads had diverged, only to come together years later.

The two of them had met again a year or so ago when her kid brother, also a cop in the LAPD, had been killed in the line of duty.

The gringo shut his eyes as he stood there. The three young men glanced at one another and started to drift away along the narrow sidewalk.

It was bad form, the man knew, to stand still in a public place with your eyes shut. You can't spot an enemy that way, the cop-commando part of him thought. But another part said nobody was liable to be after him down here, and besides, at this particular time, maybe he just didn't give a damn.

Images swam before him: visions of silky flesh, satin smooth until his touch raised gooseflesh and her breath came in little gasps interspersed with soft, high moans of life and pleasure; the exquisite woman scent of her body warmed by their desire, fueled by his caresses, driving them both to a white heat of passion...

These were the memories of just a week ago, before they had quarreled. Before the fundamental differences in their philosophies, for a while put aside by mutual agreement, had again worked their way to the surface.

At first, they thought it didn't matter. But discussions became disagreements, and disagreements became arguments that nobody could win. So finally they had called their month-long R and R quits, barely halfway through it.

He did some mental arithmetic.

That would have been three days ago, on what was probably the next to the last day of her life. Perhaps even the last day.

Maybe a guy in his line of work—counterterrorism, hard-core style—shouldn't have friends outside the team. Certainly, the blond man thought, he shouldn't have lovers. When their lives ended just because they knew you, it made for too much guilt. He didn't need those regrets.

Besides, it was kind of rough on the lovers.

Of course, she might not be who they thought at all. Kurtzman and Brognola and the Stony Man computers weren't infallible. And their information was based on what could only be called hearsay via hearsay—an informant for the Drug Enforcement Agency who told an agent, who relayed it to Stony Man Farm.

There was always the chance they were wrong.

Except that he knew, he felt they weren't.

The rugged commando with the tired eyes let the air out of his lungs in a long sigh and forced a fatalistic shrug.

He was about to find out.

**1**

Two weeks into his R and R, the Ironman was beginning to wonder if he had made a mistake. Or, more accurately, if *they* had made a mistake.

"They" were Margaret Williams and Carl Lyons, who was known to his friends as the Ironman. Depending on who you talked to, the nickname was based either on his physique—solid muscle and a constitution to go with it—or on his stubbornness. Maybe it was both.

Not that the vacation wasn't well deserved.

Lyons had just come off a particularly hairy one, a mission involving the CIA and the Russians.

It had been successful—he was still alive, and a good number of the other guys weren't—but it had left him with some kind of postcombat fatigue that gave him nightmares and a nagging suspicion that a smart man did not persist in trying to get himself killed.

The nightmares had a familiar pattern to them.

War. Conflict. Strife. A battle to the death against superior odds, numbers that he couldn't beat.

The latest one had been a real bitch.

It began as a football game. Lyons was on the field, ready for the next play. He wore full gear, tight, stretch football pants, jock, T-shirt, shoulder pads, helmet and numbered jersey. His right ankle was heavily taped and, as a result, felt stiff, inflexible. Still, all in all, he was ready, edgy and mean, willing to hit and be hit hard and to stay on his feet anyway he could.

Like Achilles, his ankle was his weakness. One time, in some fun and games in South America, his heel had taken a ricochet from a low-fired round.

He had been wearing heavy boots at the time, and the slug had fragmented and lost a good deal of its energy before it bounced. Otherwise, it would probably have taken his foot off. Still, the bullet had hit with one hell of a whap, and after that his ankle just wasn't as tight as it used to be. Most of the time, it was no sweat, but it made sense to tape his ankle before full-contact cut and run.

In the dream, everyone on the field carried guns in addition to football gear.

"Guns?" a bewildered Lyons exclaimed as they got ready to take to the field.

The old trainer nodded silently as he handed out the weapons.

"What the hell do we need guns for?" Lyons persisted. "This is football, for God's sake, not war."

"Maybe you don't know what it is," said the trainer heavily. "Maybe you just don't have any goddamn idea what you're getting yourself into."

"No shit," Lyons agreed sarcastically, thinking of all the missions he and his men went into half-blind, not really sure who the players were or who was on whose side. But that went with the territory, part of the beat, as they used to say when he was a cop. "When do we ever know that?"

"Then maybe you better just take this," snarled the trainer, holding out the guns.

Lyons shrugged and accepted the weaponry, an Uzi machine gun and a Colt Government Model .45 pistol. The latter went in a shoulder holster under his tearaway jersey; the Uzi went on a sling across his shoulder.

He had checked them expertly when the trainer handed them over. Both were loaded, ready to go.

"Spare clip?" he inquired.

The trainer shook his head. "That's all you get."

"Beautiful," muttered the Ironman. He turned and clomped out, steel cleats on scored concrete. "Not only don't they tell us what we're up against, but we go up against it with one hand tied."

They were good weapons, he knew, but they wouldn't normally be his first choice. That would have been something from the Stony Man arsenal, designed or at least reworked by "Cowboy" Kissinger, their weaponeer. But apparently only the Uzi and the government model were approved under NFL rules.

But after a while it had become clear this wasn't the NFL. This was kill or be killed.

That was typical, Lyons thought disgustedly.

A heavy fog lay over the field. It eddied and swirled in the glaring stadium lights. The mist felt like the cool hand of death against his steaming brow. The ground was covered with real turf, cold grass in a dark brown soil. For some reason, it reminded him of the lawn in a cemetery.

At the far end was a penalty box.

Lyons squinted down the field, trying to see through the shifting mist. All he could make out were the shapes of men who were standing, watching. Yet he knew without being told that these men were out of the game. Permanently out.

Then it struck him—penalty box? He turned to the referee.

"What the hell's that? This is football, not hockey. You don't have a penalty box in football, for God's sake. What's going on here?"

The referee stared at him. His eyes were dull and black. His skin was an eerie marble white above his black-and-white striped shirt. Where the stadium lights fell on it, his face glistened with a bluish tinge. His features looked stiff and somehow unmoving. When he spoke, his breath stank of death.

"Shut up, Lyons, or I'll put you in there right now."

Anger blazed in the Ironman. "I'd like to see you try!" he retorted.

The referee gazed at him, then shook his head stiffly. "You'll be there soon enough, anyway."

"Like hell!"

At Lyons's choice of words, the referee grinned a ghastly rictus. "That's right, Lyons. Exactly like hell. You'll soon know."

Lyons wanted to get a closer look at the penalty box. He walked down the sideline until he could make out the faces through the mist.

Mike Chandler was there. So were Andrezj Konzaki and April Rose. Then he saw Flor Trujillo—the sight of her cut like a knife into the scars that had formed over his grief.

"Flor!" he called. "My God, Flor!"

She didn't respond, but he had known somehow that she wouldn't. He tried again, this time with Chandler.

"Hey, Mike, buddy, what are you doing, guy? Say something, man. Talk to me, somebody!"

They still didn't answer, just gazed at him with the sad, still faces of the grave. From somewhere in Lyons's mind, a verse surfaced. God knew he made no pretense of being well-read, but for some reason it popped up anyway.

It was some lines from *Ruddigore*, by Gilbert and Sullivan. Margaret had taken him to see it only a few days before in San Francisco. It would be an excellent production, she had informed him, in that the cast included some of the members of the now defunct D'Oyly Carte Opera Company.

What the hell, Lyons had thought. And then, to his surprise, he'd found he liked it. And now, one of the scenes leaped up before him, with its howling wind, midnight skies and gray tombstones. Jesus! he thought. Why did I remember that, for God's sake? Why that and not something else?

The whistle blew a sharp blast, signaling that a play was about to get underway. Lyons gave his dead friends a long look, then turned and jogged back to the line of scrimmage.

He was playing linebacker, the ideal position for someone with his rugged power and speed. The other side had the ball; the quarterback bent over the center and began calling the signals.

"Down! Set!"

Something moved on the far sideline. Lyons glanced over.

It was the coach of the other team. He wore what looked like a long trench coat with some kind of hood attached to the collar. The mist and the glare of the lights behind him made it impossible for the Ironman to make out his face.

Lyons knew who it was, though.

The shadowy figure slowly raised an arm and pointed. The quarterback paused in calling the signals and looked over to his coach. He saw the uplifted arm, the extended bony finger, and followed the direction with his eyes.

The bony finger was pointing at Lyons.

The quarterback slowly nodded and resumed calling the play.

"Down! Set! Fifty-two, out! Ironman! Ironman! Hut! Hut!"

The line exploded into action, and then it was Lyons alone against the other team. There was no ball, no first down, just eleven men coming to kill him.

He scrabbled for the Uzi and emptied it at the rushing mass. Some went down, but others kept coming. When the machine gun locked, open and empty, he grabbed for the .45.

It wasn't there. He had lost it somewhere, somehow in the preceding plays.

With a curse, he discarded the Uzi and turned to meet the onslaught with nothing but his body and his guts to fight with.

He took the first one out with a bone-crushing blow and threw the man aside. Ditto the next one and the third and another after that. But they kept coming in waves, the other side's coach, sending in man after man, overwhelming him with sheer numbers. Now they were all around him, closing in from all directions.

Well, they could have him if they wanted, but by God, it was going to cost them. The price would be high. Maybe they'd have enough to pay it, and then again, maybe they wouldn't.

"Aaaghh!" The ragged yell tore from his throat as he braced himself against the impact of the enemy he couldn't possibly overpower.

A gentle hand touched his shoulder, and he wondered if it was Flor, welcoming him to the penalty box—had they gotten him at last? Or was it Julie, Julie Harris, the FBI agent, whom he hadn't seen since a month after the New York caper when they took out Fadi Kadal. Julie, who for the past five months had been on an undercover assignment and couldn't even make contact with family, let alone friends....

"Carl? Carl, honey, what is it? It's okay, baby, it's okay."

The field vanished, swallowed into the night mists from which it had come. Gone was the "dead of the night's high noon."

Flor was still dead.

Julie was still on her mission, and Margie Williams was holding him as he sat up in bed. His muscles were tensed, ready for battle; sweat bathed his brow and soaked the sheets around him.

He let his breath out in a ragged sigh and forced a crooked grin to his face.

"Goddamn dreams," he said weakly.

"Carl, honey, are you all right?"

"Sure." The grin was frozen on his face. "Seems real as hell while you're dreaming it, though."

Margie was a psychologist by profession. Her concern was professional as well as personal.

"Want to talk about it?" she asked softly.

Lyons shook his head.

"You sure?"

He shrugged. "Nothing to talk about, really. Just some of the bullshit floating around in my brain, I guess."

Margie sat silently for several seconds, kneading the tension from his shoulders. When she spoke, her voice was soft. "You really ought to see somebody about that, you know."

"About what?"

"The dreams. Something's not right if you're getting them like that."

"For Christ's sake, Margie!" he snapped, pushing himself up off the bed, away from her. "Knock off the touchy-feely bit, would you? I'm all right, I said."

He strode to the motel dresser and retrieved a bottle of Johnny Walker Red Label. He poured a generous slug into one of the motel's glasses and was about to knock it back in a single gulp.

Glass midway to his lips, Lyons felt the anger subside. No point in acting like a jerk, he thought. Besides, knocking back a shot of Scotch would just confirm what she was thinking. Restraining the impulse to toss it off, he took a moderate swallow and turned back to face her.

"Look, baby," he said, trying to make his voice reasonable, "it's really no big deal. I've had these dreams before, and they go away after a while." He forced a smile. "Sorry I snapped at you."

She studied him in silence for a few moments. "Why do you do it?" she asked finally.

"Do what?" He knew what she meant, of course; they had had this conversation before.

"Don't put me off," she said sharply, her eyes blazing. "Your work, of course. Kill a commie for Christ—all that stuff. Your...whatever it is." She gave a short laugh of disgust. "Junior G-man, Carl Commando."

A dozen responses leaped to his tongue. All of them were hostile, angry.

All of them were true.

I do it for those who can't do it for themselves, he thought. For all you sweet, idealistic liberals who somehow really seem to believe you can turn a sword with a smile.

I do it for my parents and for the kids I'll never have. I do it so they can live in a world where they don't have to speak Russian unless it's their choice to do so.

I do it for America, which, fucked-up though it is, is the greatest place in the world. I do it to preserve a place where damn fools—like you, Margaret, and all the others who think the enemy exists only in our paranoid minds—will have the freedom to condemn what I do.

I do it because other men and women whose opinions I respect do it, too.

I do it because it's right.

But he didn't say any of these things, mainly because it wouldn't do any good. Also, they still had two weeks together. And, apart from a few tense moments, the past couple of weeks had been pretty good. And, starting tomorrow, they were going to drive up into the wine country, the Napa and Sonoma counties of California, north of San Francisco.

Lyons had done the wine-country trip a couple of times. Both times, it had been delightful—driving from winery to winery, tasting and buying, savoring the beauty and tranquility of the rolling hills and vineyards.

Hang in there, Ironman. Get on with the trip, and it will outweigh all this bullshit. Besides, Margie means well. She's only trying to help.

Instead of trying to explain or putting his fist through the wall or walking out, he tried to dodge the issue.

"Carl Commando, huh?" he said with a grin. "Not bad. I kind of like it, actually." He took another sip of the Scotch, then walked over to the window. Pushing the heavy, light-blocking curtain aside, he gazed out over the San Francisco night.

Margie's eyes narrowed, her face hard. "Don't patronize me, dammit!"

"I'm not—"

"You think this is funny, maybe. Maybe it is. But—" her voice softened abruptly, and strangely she seemed suddenly close to tears "—but I care about you, Carl. And it hurts me to see you going around like Davy Crockett looking for an Alamo to die in."

Christ, thought Lyons, don't go mushy on me. "Or Custer looking for his Little Bighorn?" he quipped, still trying to make it light. "Horatius looking for his bridge?"

But Margaret wasn't having any of it. She turned away from him. Moments later he saw her body shaking and he knew she was crying silently.

For long moments, he looked out the window. His jaw jutted as he tried to steel himself. Her tears were a Star Wars weapon, a laser against which he was helpless. Christ, he thought, yell at me, call me a jerk, slug me, but for God's sake, don't cry.

Finally he caved in.

Moving to the bed, he knelt and put his arms around her from behind. For long moments, he held her without speaking, every sob bruising his heart like a blow from a blunt mallet, because he knew she wouldn't and couldn't ever understand.

And, worse of all, it was his fault. Or was it?

At length, she snuffled and cleared her throat. Without turning toward him, she spoke in a small voice.

"Carl?"

"Yeah?"

"I don't know why you have to do it..." She paused, trying to formulate the thought.

"Me, either."

She went on as if he hadn't spoken. "But I guess you have to do it."

"Yeah, I guess so."

"It just seems like such a waste. You've got so much, you *are* so much, and we could be so much. But you have to gamble it away. Beat it to pieces. It's like you're compelled to destroy yourself and us, too."

Lyons didn't respond.

"Oh, well," she finally mused, her voice as small as a child's, "we've got right now, anyway. But Carl?"

"Yeah?"

"After this, it's over."

"Yeah." His voice was hoarse.

"We're close, but we just don't fit somehow."

"I guess not."

"Besides—" she turned to him, her face sad and forlorn "—I don't want to be around when you finally find your last battle."

Lyons swallowed the lump in his throat. Christ, how did he ever end up in this? "Okay," he responded simply.

Suddenly she flung herself on him, clutching him, clinging to him in a gale of tears, paroxysms of grief that racked her slim body. "Hold me, Carl," she managed to gasp out. "We've still got two weeks, baby. Just hold me."

## 2

As it developed, they didn't have two weeks at all, thanks to two members of the Hell's Angels outlaw motorcycle gang and a supreme court judge.

The next day both of them made a conscious effort to put aside the past—and the future. Shortly after nine, they began winding their way toward the Napa Valley wineries.

They came to the wineries about an hour north of San Francisco. Vineyards covered the valleys and gently rolling hills like patches on a quilt. The wineries, ranging from single-family operations to huge plants, were scattered up the Napa and Sonoma valleys, linked by winding, two-lane roads.

As Lyons explained to Margaret, the idea was to go from one to the next, sampling the wines and buying whatever struck their fancy. Most of the wineries poured free tasting samples of three to ten different varieties.

"I didn't know you were an expert on wines," Margaret had observed as they set out.

"Do I look like a connoisseur?" Lyons had said, grinning. "Don't sweat it. I'm not. But I know what tastes good, and besides, most of these people are pretty nice about educating you if you're interested."

By midafternoon, they had made it to the Rocky Creek Vineyards. The proprietor, a genial gray-haired type, was expounding the virtues of the Rocky Creek cabernet, predicting that when it had aged properly—three or four years, to smooth out the oak and tannin—it would be a sure winner. Lyons didn't care about that, but he didn't mind the liberal doses the man was pouring as he spoke.

"*¡Salud!*" the proprietor announced as he finished pouring and replaced the bottle with a flourish.

"Good health and long life," said Lyons, lifting his glass.

A shriek of outrage interrupted them. It came from outside the winery building.

"What was that?" a woman in the crowd asked.

Heads turned, but only Lyons made a move to the door to check it out.

Two burly outlaw bikers had parked their choppers in the lot next to a large Mercedes sedan that had just pulled up. A portly man of about sixty and a severe-looking young woman about half that age had apparently just gotten out. Somehow, they had managed to run afoul of the bikers.

"Uh, oh," said Lyons as he took in the scene. "This could be fun," he muttered to nobody in particular.

His statement was only half-facetious. Despite his efforts to be civilized to Margie—or maybe because of those efforts—the Ironman felt in the mood for a fight.

The outlaw motorcyclists were classic examples of the species. That meant they looked as if they had crawled out from under a rock on the edge of a swamp.

One of them was a squatty, toadlike specimen with a big beard and an even bigger belly. Above the beard, his head was bald except for a fringe of stringy gray hair that sprouted and hung down from the equator of his skull. Small, piglike eyes gleamed cruelly. He looked broad and powerful, hard fat over a meaty frame.

Lyons knew the type—a "buffalo," in biker jargon. The grosser the act—gang rape, sodomy, forced oral copulation—the more it would appeal to this guy.

In contrast, his companion stood over six two, with long oily hair that hung in twisted strands like black seaweed down his back. He wasn't as thick and powerful as the toad, and his flesh had the slack, too-loose appearance of a big man who was wasting away, as though consumed by a disease. His face was pock-marked and scarred above a scraggly mustache and Vandyke beard.

Lyons glanced at the man's eyes, but he already knew what he was going to find. The wasting disease was a drug.

The biker's eyes burned with a fire that was chemically induced, his pupils contracted into dark dots. Crystal, thought the Ironman. Or crank or speed or whatever other name was in vogue for methamphetamine these days. It fit with the man's physical appearance. At one time, he had probably been a hell of a big dude, but now he was burning it away with crystal.

A "meth monster," as they used to be called back when Lyons wore a uniform.

The toad had his meaty arms around the severe-looking woman and was clutching her to him, pressing her against his gut. He wore a grease-stained black

T-shirt with a Harley-Davidson emblem on the back. The shirt rode up the man's back and sides, revealing an expanse of white-skinned fat dotted with black body hairs.

The woman struggled furiously but ineffectually to get away, emitting another shriek as Lyons and the rest of the crowd came on the scene.

The buffalo laughed in a long, dirty chuckle.

"Whazza matter, bitch? You don't like ol' Maggot?" He lifted her off the ground. She flailed her feet helplessly in the air.

Her portly companion, his face scarlet with anger, snapped an imperious command to the biker.

"Let her go this instant!"

The man wore tailored gray slacks, a pink shirt without a tie and a blue blazer. His expensive cordovan loafers had little leather tassels on the tongue in front and hanging from the heel in back. A red silk hankie protruded from the breast pocket of his blazer.

How cute, thought Lyons disgustedly, how totally fucking chic. Probably carries a little calfskin purse instead of a wallet, too. He glanced into the Mercedes and, sure enough, saw exactly that on the dashboard. The man's face looked smooth and artificially tanned beneath a dramatic shock of styled white hair.

In a word, a fop.

Lyons shook his head. Beautiful, just beautiful. Just the kind of authority figure to put these bikers back in line. Oh, well, he thought, maybe I can at least have some fun.

But there was something else, too, something that nagged at the Ironman's memory. It lay there just out of reach, something he couldn't quite identify.

Then he had it—or part of it, anyway.

He recognized the dandified wimp. He knew the guy. Somewhere, at some time in the past, he had met the old sissy. But he couldn't remember where or who the man was. Whatever the case, though, the memory did not have pleasant associations.

At the man's command, the Hell's Angel grinned. His lips pulled back to expose rotting brown-and-yellow teeth, as well as a couple of gaps where teeth weren't.

"Fuck off, asshole," he said casually.

The old dandy took a quick little step forward. "Did you hear me?" he demanded shrilly. "Release her this instant!"

The toad's eyes narrowed dangerously. Holding the woman tightly against him with his left arm, the fingers of this hand clamped painfully on her breast, he took an aggressive step forward. With his right hand, he slapped the portly man in the face, then gave a powerful shove that sent him staggering back against the Mercedes.

"I said, fuck off!" he growled.

The tall crystal freak stepped forward and pulled the man up from the ground by the front of his expensive blazer. The biker slammed his victim back against the Mercedes, then moved in close, face-to-face.

"What's the matter with you, old man?" he yelled. "Can't you hear? Get lost!"

The woman shrieked again. Lyons glanced at her and saw that the biker who called himself Maggot must have decided that he liked what his left hand had been doing with her breast. Now he was going at it with both hands, oblivious of the crowd or maybe encouraged by it.

This is bullshit, thought Lyons.

Whatever bad memories were linked with the old man, enough was enough. As he started to take a step forward, memories came back in a rush.

The sissy was Jon Rose, the chief justice of the Supreme Court of the State of California.

Pompous and self-important, Rose fancied himself witty and urbane as well as a staunch defender of the rights of criminals, never mind the victims. In short, he was a two-faced, hypocritical horse's ass. He was everything a good judge shouldn't be.

Lyons had learned about Chief Justice Rose the hard way. He checked and double-checked his memory and knew he had it right. Rose had reversed the conviction of the killer in a double murder case Lyons had handled back when he was with the LAPD.

The Ironman had caught the guy dead to rights, literally red-handed. Seeing that he was bought and paid for, the suspect had confessed. He was convicted and sent to prison for life on each murder.

Two life sentences: that meant he should have been off the streets for ten years. Maybe.

Then Chief Justice Jon Rose had gotten into the act. Lyons could still recall the exact words he had used in writing the case opinion that reversed the convictions.

Not only did Officer Lyons detain the defendant without adequate cause, but his use of force was unnecessary and unjustified. Moreover, it had the effect of so intimidating the defendant that his later admission of guilt, though undoubtedly true, may not be used as evidence at trial.

All Officer Lyons had to do was reason with the defendant before resorting to force. In any civilized society, this is a fundamental rule of life as well as of law. Because this was not done, the convictions must be reversed.

Now, looking at the portly figure in the expensive clothing, it all came back to the Ironman in a flash.

The killer had just raped and killed a twelve-year-old girl in front of her girl friend. He had clubbed her on the side of the head with a short length of pipe wrapped in black tape. Then he had raped her.

Eyes bulging with terror, the girl friend managed to rub the gag out of her mouth. She was able to scream twice for help before the suspect turned the piece of pipe on her, as well.

Somebody heard the scream and dialed 911, and Lyons was the first officer to respond. He arrived moments later and found the two pathetically small shapes sprawled on the ground.

At that moment, he knew two things.

One, he would never forget those Girl-Scout-aged faces frozen in the abject terror in which they had spent their last minutes on this earth.

Two, he was going to get this guy.

He glanced around.

The killer was nowhere to be seen.

Acting on street savvy, intuition and hunch, Lyons took off in the direction he thought the killer might have fled. In a few minutes he spotted the man, who was running across a vacant field.

The cop knew instinctively and immediately that he had the right guy.

Lyons bailed out of the car and closed the gap in a furious sprint. The killer swung a desperate sweeping blow with the pipe. It struck the Ironman's shoulder, laying open an inch-long gash. Then it was all over, and Lyons, in his words, invoked "reasonable force to effect the arrest, prevent escape and overcome resistance." Two of the killer's ribs were fractured in the process.

The man offered no further resistance. An hour later, at the hospital, he confessed in great detail to the killings. The confession was tape-recorded, and the man was fully advised of his constitutional rights.

Now, years later, ex-cop Lyons felt the same fury he had felt when the killer had first been set free by the Supreme Court. Well, now, he thought, let's see how *you* handle this, Mr. Chief Justice Rose, sir.

The Ironman had just been starting to step forward, ready to snatch Maggot the toad right out of his biker's boots. Instead, he stopped and waited.

The chief justice had seen Lyons start and then stop. "Well, come on," he demanded. "Help me subdue these animals."

Lyons looked at the woman. Pity to put her through this, he thought. But she isn't being seriously hurt yet, and besides, she chose to hang around with this liberal jerk, so she must think like he does. She'd have to—nobody else could stomach him. Hell, she's probably a public defender herself or maybe another judge.

"You're Jon Rose, chief justice of the Supreme Court," Lyons said.

The old dandy looked startled. "Why, yes, I am," he said, pleased to have been recognized. "Now, if you'll just help me with these animals . . ."

"Why don't you reason with them?" Lyons interrupted.

"Eh? What did you say?"

Lyons folded his arms across his chest and leaned against an upright post that supported the winery's second-story porch. "You heard me. This is a civilized society, isn't it? We don't want to violate Maggot's rights or anything."

"What are you talking about?" The jurist's voice rose an octave and took on a shrill edge.

"You're the police-procedure expert, aren't you?" Lyons voice was soft and sarcastic. "You're the one who decides how the cops should do it. Come on, practice what you preach. Reason with them. We don't want any of the evidence thrown out, do we?"

"My God, man. We've got to stop them. This man is committing a *crime*, for God's sake. We aren't talking about courts and lawsuits."

"Do tell," said Lyons sarcastically.

The two bikers glanced at each other. Though neither was exactly a stranger to the criminal justice system, they hadn't expected a debate on the finer points of constitutional law while they were mauling the woman.

Justice Rose glared at Lyons for a moment, then turned back to the bikers. "I said let her go!" he snapped again, but his voice had lost any element of command it had had and sounded mainly petulant and querulous. "I warn you, the consequences will be serious if..."

The tall biker slammed the jurist into the side of the car again, then kneed him in the groin. "Listen, asshole," he roared, "I'm gonna rip your head off and shit in your lungs in a minute! Now get lost!"

The old judge clutched his crotch and doubled over.

"For God's sake, Carl," snapped Margaret, "you've made your point. Do something, will you?"

The two bikers looked at her.

It was the closest thing to pure evil she had ever seen. Then the one called Maggot lifted his right hand like a gun and pointed his forefinger at her, miming a pistol.

That pissed Lyons off. Still, he returned Margaret's gaze stubbornly. "Why? This old idiot sets killers free because we didn't try to reason with them. Why should I help him?"

"Carl!" Margaret was close to tears. "Carl, will you..."

"All right, all right." Lyons stepped forward and knelt next to the jurist. "I don't think they're listening to reason, sir. Is it okay if I employ reasonable force, sir?"

The judge didn't respond.

Lyons nodded grimly and rose to his feet.

"Okay, you two dipshits, fun's over."

The two bikers glanced at each other.

"You, Maggot. Turn her loose. Now!" The Ironman's voice cracked like a whip. There was no mistaking its authority.

Maggot scowled. The taller biker looked worried. Mauling a woman or punching out a faggy-looking old liberal was evidently something the bikers could relate to. They looked like they enjoyed it, in fact. Moreover, they were good at it. Naturals, so to speak.

But the rugged blond man with the arms and shoulders was something else entirely. This wasn't the same game, and the two bikers weren't sure they wanted in on it. After all, it had been a while since they had pushed around anybody who looked that buffed out. Quite a while, in fact. If ever.

"You a cop, man?" Maggot demanded.

"Nope."

"Get lost, then! Before we kick your ass!"

"Nope."

Eyes narrowed into little slits, the toadlike biker stared at Lyons. The rugged blond man clearly wasn't intimidated. The biker decided to try a different approach.

"Hey, man, that's okay. You wanna go with us? Hack off a piece for yourself?" Rotting teeth showed in an evil grin. "She can do all three of us at the same time. Bitch'd probably like it!"

"No shit, man," chimed in the crystal freak. "That'd be bad, man. Real bad!"

The Ironman surveyed the outlaws grimly. Then he smiled.

It was a smile utterly without warmth. It held no humor. The cold, bleak change of expression only served to accent the icy gray-blue eyes.

The biker who called himself Maggot grinned back. He felt better now. This was something he could relate to, three large men gang-raping the terrified woman. And he thought the blond guy just might be going for it, too.

It was better than trying to fight him, anyway.

"Well, man," he urged Lyons, "whaddya say? You in? You wanna climb on board, buddy?"

"All three of us at once? You think she'd like it, eh?" The Ironman's smile had, if possible, become even thinner and colder than before.

The two bikers nodded eagerly.

Lyons shrugged and cocked his head to one side. "Hell, that sounds like your mom, Maggot," he goaded. "She used to like that, too."

The toad's eyes narrowed swiftly. Thrusting his face forward, he growled a command to his companion.

"Kill him, Mikey! Fuck him up good."

That was the cue Lyons had been waiting for.

The Ironman didn't wait for Mikey's response. He moved swiftly forward and grabbed the toad's free arm. With a single deft motion, he twisted it down and around in what the LAPD defensive tactics instructor had called a "pain compliance hold." With his other hand, he wrenched the girl loose from the biker's grasp.

Maggot gave a bellow of rage and pain. He jerked his arm, turning in an effort to get away from the hold. At the same time Mikey, the crystal freak, rushed in.

Lyons spun around and slammed his squatty captive against the Mercedes with a meaty smack. Then he turned to face the other biker.

"Back off!" he barked.

The tall biker froze. Now that the blond man was rid of Maggot, jumping into the fray looked considerably more risky.

By the Mercedes, Maggot was on all fours, dazed. A trickle of blood ran down his forehead onto his cheek. After a moment, he shook his head and pushed himself to his feet.

"Get him!" he roared.

Both bikers charged at once.

Maggot appeared to be the quicker of the two as well as the stronger. First things first, thought Lyons. You gotta have priorities, and Maggot was definitely priority one.

The Ironman pivoted and slammed a fist into the rushing biker's Adam's apple, then spun away and body-blocked the taller Mikey.

"Augh!"

The strangled sound tore from Maggot's throat. But he was tough and the impact only slowed rather than stopped him. As Lyons twisted to one side after body-blocking Mikey, Maggot managed an awkward but heavy blow.

It caught the Ironman just under the ear.

The buffalo had a hell of a punch.

Lyons staggered. The world seemed to darken slightly as the shock to his system shut things down a little. He knew that one or both of the bikers would be trying to tackle him, fall on him and bear him to the ground by sheer weight. And if that happened, he was in for a brutal and possibly fatal beating. . . .

He scrambled forward, trying to elude them.

Sure enough, a heavy weight hit him from behind. Lyons knew without looking that it was Mikey, brave enough at last to try a blind-side tackle.

Instead of resisting, Lyons went with the man's blow. He dived forward, using the impact to accelerate his own movement. The maneuver left Mikey clawing for Lyons's legs, rather than being squarely on top of him.

The Ironman scrabbled ahead on all fours, away from the biker's grasp. One leg came free. He pulled it up, knee to chest, then drove it backward with all the force he could muster.

Shoe sole met face with a heavy thud, accented by the crackle of nasal cartilage. Blood sprayed sideways in both directions, and the grip on Lyons's other leg came loose. He rolled free and started to come to his feet.

Out of the corner of his eye and maybe with the corner of a sixth sense, he saw it coming. But too late.

Maggot's heavy, paratrooper-style boot caught him in the chest, coming up from below in a field goal kick as Lyons was just starting to come out of his crouch.

"Mother fucker!"

Maggot's face twisted in hatred as the epithet came out in a guttural snarl.

The air exploded from Lyons in a heavy grunt as the impact hammered his body. It flashed through part of his mind that he had been lucky; Maggot had struck him with the entire top of his instep rather than with his toe. At least this way, the force of the blow was diffused over an area the size of the man's foot rather than being concentrated in a square inch or two.

Some luck, Ironman, he thought crazily. Better than nothing, though.

Again, combining principles of aikido and t'ai chi, Lyons didn't resist or oppose the blow but let himself go with it. Still the paralyzing impact flipped him over onto his back.

For a man so thick, Maggot was quick as a cat.

"Die, you cocksucker!" he roared, moving in with two more kicks as Lyons struggled for his footing. Lyons took one in the shoulder, a heavy jarring blow, while the other glanced off his face, opening a cut on his cheekbone.

In the split second before Maggot could launch his next offensive, Lyons rolled away and came to his feet.

He was still dazed, but the adrenaline was pumping full force, and he knew it was do-or-die time.

With a bellow of rage, Maggot charged.

Lyons feinted left and moved right. The biker reacted to the feint, but that was all Lyons needed. It changed Maggot's headlong plunge just far enough that Lyons was able to get off to the other side. Just enough.

Enough to avoid the charge.

Enough to put him in position to slam two quick blows from stonelike fists into the biker's kidneys as he went by, two short, explosive punches that landed just beneath his floating ribs.

Maggot went down on all fours, then arched backward, trying to twist up and rub away the paralyzing pain with one hand. Lyons circled him and made a quick snap kick into the toad's hairy white belly.

The biker went back down. Moving behind him, Lyons seized him by his greasy black T-shirt and hauled him to his feet. The Mercedes was a few feet behind them, and the Ironman spun his heavy burden toward it. Maggot slammed into the front grill and sprawled over the hood with a metallic crash. The little Mercedes hood ornament bent flat against the car's shiny finish.

Despite the pain, the buffalo instinctively pushed away from the classic arrest position.

"Kiss the hood, Maggot!" snarled Lyons, slamming him back down. The dazed biker slumped over the car.

Lyons stood there, weaving, blood trickling from the cut on his cheekbone. Gradually the ground stopped spinning, and he glanced around.

Mikey was still on the parking lot, out cold, his face in a pool of blood.

The small crowd of wine tasters was looking on in shocked silence. Margie's face jumped into focus, and Lyons read the disgust and reproach in it.

Reproach? Why, he wondered? For not jumping in sooner? For using too much force when he did jump in? For who he was and what he stood for?

Jesus, he thought, I just can't win.

Their eyes met. Instinctively he knew it was over. There would be no more wineries, no more nights of silky love. In fact, it was hard to imagine right then that there ever had been.

He broke the gaze, and scanned the crowd for the chief justice and his companion.

The woman was nowhere to be seen.

The chief justice was inside the Mercedes, doors locked, windows rolled up. He sat in the front seat, arms across his stomach, quaking.

Lyons shook his head disgustedly. He turned to Maggot. "You move, and I'll kill you. Believe me on this one."

The biker didn't move.

Lyons walked around to the driver's door of the Mercedes and knocked on the window. "It's all over, Judge. I reasoned with him and I think he understands. You can come out now."

He turned and walked to where Margie stood, her eyes glistening with tears.

"Come on, babe. Let's not throw good money after bad. I'll get you back to San Francisco. You can get a plane back home. It just wasn't meant to be, I guess."

She lowered her eyes and swallowed. Lyons looked at her, sadness and unexplainable guilt overwhelming him. Then, together, they walked slowly to their car.

3

They made the trip back to San Francisco in silence.

At first Lyons tried again to think it through. He tried to analyze what was wrong and wondered if it could ever be made right. His head throbbed from the shots he'd taken during the brawl with Maggot and Mikey. Once he stopped in a gas station and urinated, checking for blood.

There wasn't any.

To hell with it, he thought. If anything is really messed up, I'll know when it stops working. Until then, it's just like any other fight. He touched his jaw with an exploratory finger and winced in spite of himself. A present from Maggot—that first, awkward blow. One thing for sure, the bastard packs a hell of a punch, he had to admit ruefully.

Try as he might, he could come up with no better explanation for what had happened between Margaret and him than the one they already had. And that wasn't an explanation at all, merely an observation, a statement of what rather than why. *It just wasn't meant to be, I guess.*

That didn't answer anything.

Lyons replayed the tapes in his mind, reviewing and recreating their conversations and arguments a dozen times. No matter what variations he tried, the ending was the same.

As they started across the Golden Gate Bridge, Margaret suddenly turned to him. Her eyes and voice were intense with emotion. "Can't you see how wrong it is, Carl?"

"What?"

"What you do."

"I don't call what I did to those two bikers exactly wrong. What should I have done? Stood by and let them rape that girl?"

"You know what I mean," she snapped. "Stop twisting my words, damn you."

Anger flared in him. "No, I don't goddamn know what you mean." He took a deep breath, but it served only to increase rather than lessen his anger. "You know, there's just no way I can please you, is there? I hold back and let them maul her—you don't like that. I kick the shit out of them, and you don't like that, either. Well, honey, maybe you'll be so good as to *tell* me how to play it, 'cause I'm sure as hell at a loss."

She glared at him through narrowed eyes. "It's all so easy for you, isn't it?" she said contemptuously. "Good guys and bad guys. If you're not one, then you must be the other."

"Is that so wrong?" asked Lyons, a trifle bewildered.

"Yes, it's wrong. It's wrong in a way you could probably never understand."

"Try me."

She shook her head. "It's an oversimplification, and it's not accurate. The world isn't like that."

Lyons still didn't understand what her fundamental complaint was. "Maybe it is and maybe not," he admitted, "but as a way of life, it works okay most of the time." His voice softened as he began to see beneath the smoke. "But that's not it, is it? Oversimplification or whatever isn't really what's bothering you."

He glanced over at her as he drove. In that brief second the anger in her face seemed to melt. The hard lines of emotion crumbled, and then she was crying, not looking at him, tears running unchecked down her cheeks.

"It's killing us," she said. "You're destroying us. We could make it if it weren't for that. But you can't let go, can you?"

"Margie, that's *me*. That's what I do. Hell, that's what I *am*. If that's why we can't make it, then that's the way it is." And, he thought, that's the way it was fifteen years ago when we couldn't make it then, either.

She spoke as if she'd read his mind. "Maybe that's what we figured out way back when," she said in a small voice. "Only we just forgot it."

"Maybe so," he agreed softly.

"You know, I've always loved you, in a way. In spite of our differences. I've always known you're the best man I could ever have. Better than anybody else out there."

Christ, thought Lyons, don't do this to me. "Knock that shit off," he said clumsily. "Maybe you just think you love something else that isn't me."

She ignored him. "But there's something there that means it just won't work, isn't there? Something in you that makes it doomed to failure." She turned suddenly and looked at him, her face hard and forceful. "This is it, you know. I can't take it. I may always love you—part of me will, anyway—but I'll never see you again.''

He nodded, a lump in his throat. There wasn't anything left to say.

They drove through San Francisco to the airport, which was some twenty minutes south of the city.

Lyons parked the car in the massive concrete parking structure north of the main terminal. He unlocked the trunk and removed her bags.

''Are you just going straight back to L.A.?'' he asked, his voice cordial but formal.

She shook her head. ''There's a conference, a symposium actually, of clinical psychologists in New Orleans. I think I'll go there.''

''It's going on right now?''

She nodded, rummaging in her purse for something.

''Will you be able to get in?''

''What? Oh, yeah. In fact, I signed up for it six months ago, before this—our trip—came up. I never canceled the reservations.''

''Well,'' he said, bending and picking up her bags, ''it shouldn't be too hard to find a direct flight there.''

She made a negative gesture toward the luggage. ''I can get these inside by myself. You can just take off if you like.''

He shook his head. ''No, I *don't* like. At least let me get you on the goddamn plane, will you?''

Now it was her turn to be cordial. ''Sure, Carl.''

Twenty minutes later she had a direct flight on United to New Orleans. Departure time was in thirty-five minutes.

The bags checked, Lyons walked her down the shabby tunnel toward the boarding gate, stopping short of the metal detectors. She turned toward him, a plastic smile fixed bravely on her face.

"I guess this is it, isn't it?" she said with forced brightness.

"Yeah, I guess so."

"Thanks for the help with the bags."

"No sweat."

They stood awkwardly, both aware there was nothing left but the goodbyes that had to be said, but neither willing to start it.

Suddenly she reached impulsively up to him and clamped her arms around his neck. She pulled him down and kissed him hard on the mouth. When they separated, her face twisted into a smile.

"For what was," she said. "And for what almost was."

"Yeah."

"And maybe for what can never be."

"Yeah." Christ, I'm in a rut, he thought. Can't I find something better than that to say?

"I better get going."

He nodded. Instinctively he said, "See you later."

She shook her head. "No. Goodbye."

He knew what she meant. "Goodbye, then."

As she started to turn away, he called after her. "Margaret?"

"Yes?"

He cleared his throat. "You know..." He swallowed. "You know, if you ever need anything, anything along the lines of what I do—" he gave a wry smile and made a clumsy attempt to be light-hearted

"—you know, assassinations, bridges blown up, that sort of thing—I hope you'll call for me."

She gave him a long look but didn't respond. He went on.

"You've got the number. They can always get to me if I'm anywhere I can be gotten to." The number he referred to would get her, after a number of call-forward jumps and back checks, directly to Brognola or the Bear, Aaron Kurtzman, at Stony Man Farm.

She still didn't say anything.

"Well, Christ, Margaret," he blurted awkwardly, "like I said, it's what I am, what I do. I don't have anything else I can give you, so I'm giving you that. You need me—somebody's giving you trouble nobody else can handle—call me. I'll come if I can. And if I can't, somebody else will." His voice softened. "I know it's goodbye, babe. I'm just leaving you a string on it—in case of emergency, you know?"

Finally she nodded. "I know," she whispered. "Thanks, Carl."

"Yeah." He looked down at the worn carpet. When he looked up, she was passing through the metal detector. She reclaimed her bag and strode down the tunnel to the boarding gate.

## 4

Delbert Gunther rose from his crouch and stepped up quickly behind the uniformed guard at Gate C of the Nuclear By-Products Storage Facility in Louisiana.

He called it the four-step knife kill. It never failed. All he had to do was avoid the sweep of the video camera; the rest was automatic.

When the camera panned slowly past, the killer knew he had twenty-two seconds, more than enough time.

Four steps. He knew them by heart.

One!

With his powerful left arm, he reached around the unsuspecting victim and clamped a vicelike fist over the man's mouth. Animal strong, he levered the guard's head back, smothering the startled grunt with the palm of his hand and the force of his attack.

Two!

He held the knife in his clenched fist, blade protruding from the top of his hand. The hilt was butted up tightly against his thumb and forefinger—one of the characteristics of a dagger, he knew, was a handguard or the sharp narrowing of the grip to prevent the user's hand from sliding forward onto the blade if the knife hit bone or hard meat.

As Sergeant Drago used to say at one of the mercenary camps Gunther attended, "It's always embarrassing for the cutter to get cut up along with the cuttee."

Gunther jammed the dagger into the man's back with his right hand. He made it a solid, powerful blow, driving the blade clear up to the hilt. Sharp steel pierced the man's kidneys, slicing the nerve-filled tissue and causing instantaneous shock. The guard stiffened, his body going into paralyzed rigidity. He died without a sound.

Three!

The killer gave a brutal twist to the knife, then yanked it back out. Blood streamed from the rent in the flesh.

Time to make sure. Whatever's worth doing at all is worth doing well, he thought, suppressing a giggle. If only Miss Amos, his grade three teacher, who'd considered such proverbs a way of life, could see him now.

Four!

He reached around and up high to slit the man's throat.

Still twisting the guard's head back with his left hand, Gunther plunged the cruel knife into the exposed and unprotected neck. Silently, savagely, he yanked the blade from left to right, laying open the throat with a hiss of steel on flesh. Blood fountained and spattered on the gray cement.

Red on gray—how stylish, he thought.

He dragged the dead man off the concrete roadway and glanced in both directions. All clear. Ahead, beyond a heavy gate made of steel and chain link and topped with razor wire, lay the target: the major nuclear-waste disposal facility in Louisiana, one of the most secret in the country. It was protected by two concentric perimeter fences and an armed security force at the facility itself.

Correction, thought Gunther.

Make that *one* perimeter fence now. Whoever had designed the security had made it easy for him; this particular gate was not visible from either the inner fence or the facility control. As long as he avoided the video camera, it was no sweat.

The camera swept slowly toward him.

Gunther dragged his burden toward the camera, hauling the dead man under it, crouching in the cone-shaped blind spot beneath the electronic eye. The camera moved on by. Twenty-two more seconds, he thought, while it swept the other direction and returned.

NEARLY A MILE AWAY, in a steel building inside the inner perimeter fence, another armed guard sat at a metal desk. On the wall before him were six video monitors, six television sets, each hooked to a different camera.

The guard was reading a paperback, trying to fight the boredom of his job by escaping into the pages of men's adventure.

"Whatcha reading, Hal?" The question came from the other man in the building, another guard.

The guard named Hal looked up. "Huh? Oh, this. Blood-and-guts stuff, that's all."

The other guard's eyes drifted from the book to the video monitor for Gate C. "Hey!" he exclaimed.

Hal turned to follow his companion's gaze. "What is it?"

"Gate C."

"What about it?"

"Where's Charlie?"

Hal stared at the screen. Sure enough, the scene was missing the familiar shape of the large man normally on guard there during this shift. The two men watched as the camera panned slowly on by.

Still no Charlie.

"Think we should check it out?"

Hal considered it, then shook his head. "Naw, guy's probably just taking a leak. Probably shaking it out right now. If he ain't there next couple of passes, then we'll take a look." He turned back to his book.

THE KILLER WORKED busily over the dead man whose uniform consisted of a navy jump suit with white shoulder patches. A Sam Browne belt and holster of smooth black leather held a .45 on the right side and spare clips and a hand-held radio on the left.

The shoulder patches had four letters stitched in red on the white background: NBSF. The initials stood for Nuclear By-Product Storage Facility.

The NBSF was in Louisiana's wild back country. Huge canisters of radioactive death were tucked here and buried in the perpetual dryness of the abandoned salt mines.

Each one as big as a petroleum tank car, the containers came from nuclear reactors and power plants all over the country. The multilayered canisters contained different mixtures of nuclear substances. Some held uranium 235, the rare and highly fissionable isotope best suited to the nuclear chain reactions required for reactors. Others contained plutonium, uranium 238 and 239, and neptunium 93.

Their controlled fissions completed, the products all had one thing in common. They were deadly—hot with gamma and beta rays—and would remain that way for a century or two, interred in isotopic isolation in the dry, stable tombs of the old salt mines.

Like Count Dracula, they were perfectly harmless as long as they lay undisturbed in their special alloy coffins. But once released, it would be a different story.

Burn, baby, burn, thought Gunther, I'll set you free.

He recalled how disgusted he had been to learn how the facility came by its name. It had originally been called NWDF, which stood for Nuclear Waste Disposal Facility. But because of the weakness that had infiltrated every level of America, the name had been changed to something that was more politically palatable.

Fags and commies, he thought.

So "waste" became "by-product," and "disposal" became "storage." It was all to avoid the phony hysteria created by the media over nuclear power—hysteria now linked in the minds of the public to the term *nuclear waste*.

What a country of pussies America had become, the killer thought disgustedly. Well, that was about to change, and he was the guy to do it....

Gunther bent over the dead man at his feet and swiftly grabbed the zipper that ran up the front of the jump suit from crotch to throat. He pulled it down and hauled the navy garment off the body. Blood soaked the area where the knife had gone into the man's back, but the fabric was so dark that the stain wasn't really noticeable. He recalled an old joke about how doing a good job was like wetting your pants while wearing a dark suit; it gives you a warm feeling, but nobody really notices.

Gunther giggled again. He knew he had done a good job with the knife. "Did this give *you* a warm feeling, pal?" he whispered to the dead guard.

The man didn't answer.

Moments later Gunther was dressed in the jump suit and the other equipment, including the dead man's leather gear, gun and radio. Keeping his face away from the video camera, Gunther walked confidently back into its range and assumed what he hoped would look like a posture of watchful vigilance while he waited for the next phase of the operation to begin.

Killing the unsuspecting guard had given him a warm, almost-sexual flush of pleasure. One thing was for sure, the technique never failed.

He had learned it three years ago at the Mercenary Operations School, a private, soldier-of-fortune outfit that specialized in taking money in return for teaching the manly arts of homicide and mayhem. Gunther had attended several mercenary schools and soon discovered that most were very basic or were outright frauds. Most of the "instructors" had been fakes, too, guys who stood around in fatigues and mirrored shades, "lookin' cool."

But Sergeant Drago, the hand-to-hand combat instructor at MOS, was different.

He'd been there, and he'd done it all. It was worth putting up with all the bullshit and rip-offs to find somebody like Drago. And, Gunther knew, the instructor was as pleased to find a guy like himself, a real man who wasn't afraid to do what had to be done.

"It's just like anything else," Sergeant Drago had said. "Ya gotta work on it till it's automatic. Grab, stab, pull back and slice. One, two, three, four. Ya do it right, and it never fails."

Gunther liked the simplicity of Drago's approach.

He practiced for hours on life-size dummies. One— grab. Two—stab. Three—pull back. Four—slice. It gave him a feeling of power, of being somehow special.

Gunther liked to think about the four steps whenever he had to be around somebody who thought he was hot shit.

Usually it would be an important person or some guy who thought he was bad or cool. Maybe the dude would be showing off, flashing money, talking big, being tough. Doctors and lawyers, especially lawyers, the self-important two-faced pricks. And the athletes, especially the blacks, with money and fame and white women all over them. Del didn't like guys like that. They got on his nerves. And when that happened, he just remembered Sergeant Drago and his four-step knife-kill method.

I could take you out right now, he would think. You're mine, anytime I want you, you prick. It made him feel better.

But that was all practice, he thought as he looked down at the dead guard. This is the real thing.

The jump suit was too tight across the shoulders, though in other respects it fit well enough. The dead guard had been six two, only an inch shorter than Gunther, but the guard had lacked the killer's powerful physique. Still, it would have to do. Gunther moved his meaty shoulders, then unfastened the snaps on the chest above where the zipper ended. That gave him a little more room.

Gunther weighed in at a solid 240. Damn little of it was fat.

His hair and his beard were light brown, nearly blond. His eyes were an intense blue. He was handsome, or would have been, except that there was something wrong about his face. It wasn't any one feature exactly; it was more that something was missing, something indefinable, which by its absence, made him look less than human, somehow evil.

He had played college football at Louisiana State University. After that he had devoted his time to right-wing politics and bar fights.

Gunther regarded the bar fights as both fun and good practice. He worked as a bouncer at the Star and Garter, a strip club in New Orleans. He had won Louisiana's unofficial World's Strongest Bouncer contest two years in a row. The word among the bar crowd was that the guys who got out of hand at the Star never went to jail . . . without going to the hospital first.

On the political front, Delbert Gunther started with the John Birch Society and progressed to the Ku Klux Klan. Ultimately he'd abandoned both.

"Wimps," he once explained, "they're nothing but a bunch of pussies. They talk a big fight but don't do shit about actually changing anything."

Accordingly he set out to find a group that was more militant and, if possible, more politically extremist. When he discovered there wasn't really anything to the right of these two groups, he took matters into his own hands and started his own group: ARC. The letters stood for Aryan Right Coalition.

Later he came to realize that most people, especially of the type he wanted to attract, whose beliefs were like his, didn't know what *Aryan* meant. When that happened, Del adopted a nickname for the group that was more straightforward and less easily misunderstood.

The White Right.

Gunther was no dummy. He had studied—and generally misinterpreted—the writings of the German philosopher Friedrich Wilhelm Nietzsche. It was from Nietzsche that he had learned of the concept *Übermensch*, the great philosopher's idea of the ultimate in man's evolution, a class of overlords destined to rule the lesser peoples.

Guys like himself.

From there, he had proceeded to study various teachings of Adolf Hitler. Hitler, he decided, was a prophet in whose wisdom lay man's only hope for survival. Nazi dogma taught him the term *Aryan* as misused to refer to pure white peoples, free from any hint of either nonwhite or Jewish blood.

The more he read, the more he recognized his calling.

Then came the day when Gunther carried his white-supremacy philosophy into action. That was the same day he first tried out Sergeant Drago's four-step knife-kill method for real.

The guy had been a real scumbag, a mid-Easterner of some sort.

Gunther knew the type. Rag heads. Camel jockeys. Sand greasers. By any name, polluters of the white race. And, to top it off, the guy had been with a white woman. The couple's car, a Porsche, had broken down along a deserted stretch of highway.

Gunther despised the woman as much as the man. Maybe more so. She was a whore, fornicating like that with the lower races.

The World's Strongest Bouncer pulled his van to the shoulder on the pretext of offering help.

"What's the problem, partner?" he asked in his best good-ol'-boy drawl. It worked, he thought exaltedly, the camel jockey was fished in completely.

When the man turned to point to something in the car, Gunther glanced up and down the highway.

Nobody in sight.

Ignoring the girl, Gunther went into autokill. His mind had been programmed by Sergeant Drago, and his body obeyed. He was a supreme killing machine, and nothing could stop him.

He was an *Übermensch*.

Sergeant Drago was right. It worked like a charm. Gunther still remembered the tightening in his groin as the knife went into the man's back. It was better even than being with a woman, which had never been that much fun anyway, Gunther thought.

The girl had been even better. Her terror and abject supplication had fired him with a killing lust that was more satisfying by far than any sex he had ever had.

Two years had gone by since then. The police never solved the killings. The homicides were the work of a madman, a serial killer perhaps, they said. Such crimes were the toughest of all to solve, because there was no motive to the killings.

Gunther knew better. The man and his whore had died because they deserved to die, and because in a small way, they were the first step toward the purification of the Aryan race.

Now, as he looked down at the dead guard at his feet, Gunther grunted in satisfaction. The man was in a way another first step, albeit a giant one in comparison with the first killing.

When this mission was over, an angel would be born.

An angel to purify the races. An angel of—Gunther giggled as he thought of it—radiant beauty. An angel born of his own efforts here in these Louisiana salt mines.

His Cajun angel.

And what better place for his creation to begin her holy work than New York City? With its melting-pot population, its crime-ridden ghettos, it was the ultimate cesspool for the corruption of white racial purity.

An official-looking van pulled up to where Gunther stood. It was light blue, and bore the seal of the State of Louisiana. Inside were four men, each dressed in khaki coveralls and wearing the red baseball cap of the Louisiana State Department of Hazardous Materials.

The uniforms were fake. The truck was a fake. The credentials that each carried—if there had been anyone to check them—were also fake. Each man was a sworn and trusted member of the Aryan Right Coalition, the White Right.

Each was also a killer.

The door along the right side of the van slid open, and Gunther heaved the body of the dead guard inside. Then, as the video camera panned back across them, he reached for the hand-held radio on the Sam Browne belt, keyed the mike and spoke confidently into it.

"Gate C to Control."

The radio crackled in his hand. "Control here. Go ahead, Gate C."

"I have a vehicle here from the State Department of Hazardous Materials. Something about an inspection."

"Control here. That's a negative, Gate C. Only inspectors allowed here are feds, NRC."

Gunther knew the Nuclear Regulatory Commission had primary jurisdiction over the plants. It was all part of the act.

"Ten four, Control. I'll check it out." He turned off the radio for several moments, then came back on the air. "Gate to Control. Subject says he's supposed to meet NRC inspectors here. Part of a project on HazMats control, that's all."

HazMats was the commonly used abbreviation for hazardous materials.

There was a pause on the other end. Then the radio crackled again. "Ten four, Gate C. That makes sense. Escort them through."

"Roger, Control. Gate C out."

Planning is everything, thought Gunther exultantly. It started with the careful monitoring of the facility's radio traffic to learn the procedures. It included getting the van, an exact duplicate of the actual state vehicles, and even went so far as a telephone call to the control staff of the facility, informing them the feds from NRC and the locals from the Louisiana State Department of Hazardous Materials would be doing a joint study later that day.

The gate swung open, its electrical locks activated from the main control station. The van pulled through and Gunther climbed into the passenger's seat.

A quarter of a mile later, beyond a rise, was another fence similar to the first one. The van slowed as another uniformed guard came out to meet them. Already, Hal, or the other guard in the main facility, had pulled the switch to open the gate; Gunther heard the sharp electric click of the lock being activated and saw the gate open.

Gunther waved to the man from inside the cab of the truck.

Instinctively the guard started to wave back. Then, abruptly, he stopped, his brow knitting as he saw the unfamiliar face.

"Hey! Where's Charlie? I thought Charlie was working the gate today."

Gunther leaned out of the truck and looked down at the suspicious guard. "Charlie's not here," he replied with a warm, friendly smile.

"Where is he?" the other man demanded, uncertain what to do.

"Charlie isn't anywhere. Not any more. Charlie checked out. Poor Charlie," said Gunther, still smiling.

By this time the video camera had swung on by. Gunther smiled even more broadly and shot the man in the head.

He used a silenced .22, a Ruger target pistol. The semiautomatic weapon had been carefully fitted with a silencer and was loaded with high-speed .22 long-rifle hollowpoints. The small bullet, moving about two thousand feet per second, drilled through the center of the man's forehead, killing him instantly.

Gunther sprang from the truck and hauled the dead man to the rear of the vehicle, out of sight of the returning camera. He heaved the body on top of the corpse of the first guard, then strode ahead and swung the gate open.

The van pulled through, and Gunther climbed back inside.

A clearing of perhaps five acres lay before them. A chain link fence eight feet high and topped with two feet of razor wire ringed the compound, but the gate was wide open. In the front right quadrant, at about five o'clock, was a steel butler building about the size of two average two-story homes pushed against each other. Several pieces of heavy equipment—cranes, trucks, half-tracks and Caterpillar bulldozers—were parked in an orderly manner near the steel structure.

"Look there." Gunther pointed beyond the butler building to the entrance to the salt mines. "The trucks."

Parked near the back of the compound, a couple of hundred yards behind the steel building, were three semis, the tractors hooked to rigs carrying nuclear-waste canisters. Apart from the triangular nuclear warning signs and various other hazardous materials insignia, the semis looked for all the world like the tank trucks used to haul gasoline or milk.

Anticipation washed over Gunther like a wave. Inside the steel containers lay the life force of his creation, his Cajun angel.

The van swung into the parking area adjacent to the main steel building. The driver and two of the passengers got out and strode confidently to the door. This time, Gunther remained inside so that the man or men who came to the door wouldn't see that he wasn't Charlie from Gate C.

The door opened, and the guard named Hal stepped out.

"Mornin', fellas," he began.

They were his last words. The driver took out a silenced .22 pistol and calmly raised it. The guard froze, then started to cry a warning and go for his own weapon at the same time.

He never made it.

The initiator's advantage belonged to the killer from the White Right. With a single harsh cough, the pistol dispatched it's tiny missile of death. The guard slumped to the ground.

The two men who had gotten out with the driver burst into the steel building. The second guard, still lounging in a chair, jerked his head around in surprise.

"Freeze!" snapped one of the attackers.

The guard froze.

"Hands behind your head, fingers laced together!"

Trembling, the guard complied. "Now, on your knees!" barked the intruder.

When Delbert Gunther entered the room, the frightened captive was kneeling on the floor, facing the wall, his hands locked behind his head, his .45 in the possession of Gunther's partner.

"Why didn't you kill him?" inquired the White Right leader.

"We thought you might like to do that."

Gunther nodded. "Good thinking." He took out his own silenced .22 and calmly shot the man in the back of the head. The body spasmed forward against the wall and subsided limply onto the floor.

The door opened and the fourth phony HazMats man entered. "Hey, Del," he began.

Gunther silenced him with a sharp wave of his hand. For several moments, they stood quietly, listening, and scanning the video monitors for any sign that they had been discovered. Finally Gunther allowed himself a slight smile. He hadn't expected it to be so easy, though he knew that the successful ones were the ones that went smoothly.

"Yeah, man," he said. "What were you sayin'?"

"Where's the stuff?"

"Out back." Gunther indicated the direction with a jerk of his head. "Let's get going."

Two minutes later they had located the right truck—the one loaded with U 235. The isotopes were carefully shielded, the container trapping the deadly gamma and beta rays in the layers of lead and other inert materials.

"Beautiful," Gunther murmured. "Burn, baby, burn."

The men fell to work. All the nuclear and HazMats insignia came off the truck. A large, bright blue magnetic sign that read Atlantic Richfield Company was affixed to each side of the tank on the trailer. New license plates, new Interstate Commerce Commission papers, new trucker's logs, all went into place.

In ten minutes the truck was indistinguishable from any other ARCO truck hauling gasoline.

In twenty minutes, it was pulling onto the highway, bound for New York.

Delbert Gunther surveyed their handiwork.

"Well done, boys," he murmured. "Well done, indeed."

The purification was beginning. Two of his men would drive the truck out of the compound and head toward New York. At a rest area some sixty miles away, they would be relieved by a couple of bikers from California who'd been supplied by a friend of Gunther's in Oakland.

The bikers wouldn't know what they were pulling, but they would know enough not to ask questions. And, if anything went sour, it couldn't be traced back to Del.

He checked his watch. Time to get going to meet his drivers at the airport.

The war had begun.

5

The United Airline's 747, flight 823, touched down at 5:43 p.m. and taxied toward the terminal. "We ask that you remain in your seats until the aircraft has come to a complete stop. We hope you have a pleasant stay in New Orleans, and thank you for flying United."

The flight attendant flashed a neon smile and replaced the microphone. Then, ignoring her own advice to remain seated, she and her colleagues busied themselves cleaning the small galley and taking inventory of the food items served.

In the back of the plane, a broad, squatty man pushed himself to his feet and stepped into the aisle.

He wore filthy jeans and a leather vest, the uniform of the hard-core outlaw motorcycle gangster, and he moved with a certain stiffness, as though there were parts of his body he didn't want to bend. From the adjacent seat, his companion, who was a good deal taller but just as dirty, gazed out the scratched plastic window.

The two men smelled as good as they looked.

Maggot elbowed his way into the aisle in front of a pleasant-looking woman with spectacles and snow-white hair. She gave an indignant gasp of protest, and the biker wheeled abruptly to face her.

"You got a problem, old woman?" he snarled.

The lady blinked and almost lost her balance as she stepped back from the biker. Maggot glared balefully at her, an unreasonable hatred welling within him. He wished he could just jam his knee into her soft, elderly belly and then kick some ribs when she fell....

Maggot didn't feel good.

His head throbbed and his body ached. His left eye was swollen nearly shut. The eyelid resembled an eggplant or an overstuffed chair upholstered in purple. That eye hurt even when he blinked the other one, the movement sending sharp pains shooting through already sensitive nerves. The lower right corner of his jawbone felt even worse. Whenever he opened his mouth to speak or eat, the joint grated as if its socket were lined with ground glass. A thick swelling ran down the length of his jaw and underneath it; swallowing was as uncomfortable in its own way as blinking his eyes.

And his ribs. Jesus, his ribs.

The blond guy's fists had been like stones or even worse. Maggot, who was no stranger to fist city, could only recall being hit that hard once before in his life.

Years back, he had gone elk hunting in Idaho. At the time, he had just gone AWOL from the army and was on the run. An old buddy had arranged the trip, and they had packed in on horseback under the care of one of the best guides in the state.

After two days without even a sighting, they came across a small herd. It was commanded by a magnificent bull elk, a big bastard, one of the biggest even the guide could recall seeing.

In the prime of its life, well fed from a good season on the mountain ranges, the stag was tall and heavily muscled. A majestic rack of antlers crowned the proud beast.

The hunters pulled up, and Maggot's buddy tossed a coin. The toss went to him, and he got the first shot.

And blew it. In a burst of explosive power, the bull galloped away unharmed. "You blind son of a bitch," growled Maggot at his buddy. "Next shot's mine. He won't get away again."

The next day they came across the same herd, protected by the same bull elk. Maggot rested his 7.62 autoloader on a rock and let fly.

Like his buddy had the day before, Maggot missed on the first shot. And the second and the third. But unlike his buddy, he kept shooting as the elk bounded away. Oblivious of the danger of a wounded animal, he emptied the clip.

And he got lucky.

One of the slugs hit the elk in the foreleg, just below the knee. It all but shot the limb off. Another round hit the flank. It was a placement that was unlikely to knock the animal down. Moreover, it wouldn't draw enough blood to make tracking easy. Still, the animal would probably die in agony within a few hours or, at most, a day or two.

All in all, it was precisely the kind of shot that no real hunter makes.

The combination of the two shots put the proud beast down, though. They saw its hind end buckle and then collapse, but the beast struggled to regain its feet. Finally it subsided onto the hillside, flat on its side and lay with its eyes closed, motionless.

"I told ya', man," Maggot bragged to his friend as he swaggered up to his kill. "I told ya' he wouldn't get away from *me*."

The guide started to speak. The fact that the elk's eyes were closed meant it was probably still alive. But the crude, bullying braggadocio of the squatty deserter was rubbing the old cowboy the wrong way, and he decided to remain quiet.

"Just look at this bastard," Maggot gloated. "Biggest goddamn elk in the whole place, I'll bet." He stepped up to the downed beast and grabbed the antlers, twisting them and lifting the head of his trophy.

That was a mistake.

Despite its shattered front leg and the gut shot, the elk exploded into action. In a massive spasm of animal power, it heaved upward and scrabbled to its feet. Maggot, who had been straddling the beast to lift its antlers, ended up momentarily draped over its neck and shoulders. Then, with a twist that would put a rodeo bronc to shame, the elk heaved the squatty deserter onto the hillside and wheeled to take flight.

In the process, it gave Maggot a single, powerful, straight-back kick with one of its hind feet.

Flint-hard hoof struck the meaty portion of Maggot's upper back, just to one side of his backbone.

The jolt of pain hit hard and hurt deep. For some reason, the pain seemed to begin somewhere inside his body. It welled and radiated outward, and Maggot was left with a bruised back and injured insides. It had hurt for weeks.

That was the only other time that Maggot could recall being hit as hard as the blond man had hit him the day before. And he could tell that he would hurt as long this time as he had from the elk.

One thing would be different, though.

The elk had gotten away. Somehow, despite its crippling wound, the proud beast had bounded away along the hillside. By the time the guide and Maggot's friend got their rifles out, it had vanished into the rugged mountains to die as it had always lived—on its own terms.

Whatever it took, Maggot wasn't going to let that happen again. The blond guy would pay.

From the window seat, Mikey had not seen his friend's exchange with the lady in the aisle. A drug-induced paranoia raged within the tall biker. He had been doing lines of crystal methamphetamine around the clock, speeding his metabolism to the red line. It killed his appetite, though he needed food; it kept him awake and hyper, though he needed sleep. These days, feeling good just meant not feeling too bad, and the only way to do that was to do more meth.

Like a building in which the occupants were tearing wood off the walls to burn for fuel, Mikey's body was being consumed from within. And, as his body broke, his mind bent.

His vision separated.

He could be looking at something, like the Delta airliner waiting for the take-off signal on the next runway, and one moment, everything would be sharp and focused, a bright brittle image on his brain. The next moment, the image would start to split, dividing as if each of his eyes were working independently. One airplane would become two. Then images would move apart, one to the right and the other to the left, bisecting his brain.

His mind raged.

Images of the past, all bad episodes, flashed across his consciousness. Two and a half years in a federal penitentiary for racketeering. Putting a hatchet into his girlfriend's head. The petrochemical stench of napalm laid down from the air on the jungles of Vietnam. The blond guy yesterday and the woman who had been with him.

Cops. The law.

They had to be. The guy handled himself too well to be anything else. Look at the way he slammed Maggot over the hood of the car. Mikey had been on the receiving end of enough arrests to recognize the position. The woman, the classy-looking bitch with the short brown hair, she didn't look like a cop, exactly. Still, she was with the guy. She was probably a federal agent of some kind. A narc, maybe. FBI or DEA, he thought.

Whatever the agency, they were cops, all right. And they were after him.

Having cops after them could mean only one thing. Prison. And that was out of the question. He couldn't do it again. Just no fucking way. He'd cut a baby's throat if that's what it took to stay out of the joint.

He wondered if he could do a line right now. Just a small one, to get him going again.

Something jabbed him in the side of the head. For an instant, Mikey was only a hair away from going berserk. Then he realized it was only Maggot.

"Hey, jerk off, let's move it." The squatty biker bent forward to poke Mikey in the head again. Anger blazed in him, and he knocked Maggot's hand away with a jerky swat of his arm. Maggot pulled quickly back.

The movement caused pain to sheer through Maggot's back, and he grunted involuntarily. "I'll kill that blond bastard," he muttered through clenched teeth, oblivious of the cautious stares of the other passengers in the crowded aisle.

Ten minutes later, they were limping through the crowded terminal.

"How are we gonna get there?" asked Mikey at last. His lips were dry and cracked. White flecks of dried spittle lodged in the corners of his mouth.

"Supposed to be a dude in a red pickup outside someplace. Some big-shot brother in the White Right, I guess."

"Then what?"

"Shit, man, I don't know any more than you do," Maggot snarled. "They got a tractor rig we gotta drive to New York, that's all."

"What for?"

"How the hell do I know what for?" Anger flared in Maggot's voice, fueled by the throbbing in his back. "'Cause Filthy Dave said so, that's what for."

Filthy Dave was the president of the Oakland chapter of the band of bikers that Maggot and Mikey belonged to. A cruel and massive buffalo of a man, he ruled the club with an iron fist: what he said went. No questions invited and none answered.

Maggot winced. Showing his anger was a mistake; his face was still too tender for that. "Anyway, some dude back here called Dave an' asked for a coupla guys to help out an' shit, an' Dave gets me and says you an' me are goin' to do it. That's all I know."

"And so we're drivin' this rig to New York?"

"Yep."

"What's in it?"

Maggot shrugged. "Gas, he said."

The taller biker shook his head. "I don't like it, man. It sucks. Rig's probably hot, and we'll end up in the joint again."

"You wanna call up Filthy Dave and tell him you ain't gonna do it? He'll knock your ass out for sure. An' that's just for starters, man."

Mikey didn't respond.

"Besides, we get caught, they'll take care of us. Get us a couple of tight-ass lawyers, dick the case around for six months or a year, easy. By the time it's done, we don't do shit in custody. Come on. Let's move it."

But Mikey wasn't listening.

The tall, wasting biker stood frozen, his gaze fixed on something across the wide lobby that led to the baggage claim area.

It wasn't that they had any luggage to pick up. The two bikers traveled light, carrying nothing but the clothes on their backs and several heat-sealed plastic bags of crystal methamphetamine stitched into the seams of their leather jackets which sported the colors of their club. But now Mikey stood transfixed, gazing toward the merry-go-round device that was disgorging luggage like crumbs scattered on a long metal tongue.

"No."

The word came out as a whisper. He repeated it, stretching it into a long, harsh sound of desperation and supplication.

"Noooo!"

Mikey's eyes blazed, and his body took on a peculiar rigidity. The image kept separating, dividing and drifting apart, the way the Delta jet on the next runway had been doing. He tilted his head to one side, the muscles in his neck rigid and stiff. He tensed his forehead, trying to force the images back together, to make them merge into a single person again.

It worked but only for a second, and then the image started to slide apart again. But whether it was one image or two, there was no mistaking who it was.

He still couldn't believe it. He looked again to be sure.

No doubt about it. It was tne woman with the short dark hair, the one who had been with the blond guy at the winery. The one who had to be a cop of some kind, a federal agent maybe.

She was here! Yesterday, fifty miles north of San Francisco. Today, New Orleans. It didn't occur to him that the woman and her male companion had been at the winery *before* he and Maggot had arrived. In his pharmaceutical paranoia, it wouldn't have mattered. The cops were everywhere, and they were closing in on him.

Eyes bulging, he stared, looking for the blond guy. No luck—the bastard was probably hidden. And the bitch was trying to look innocent, talking at the baggage assistance counter.

"Whazza matter, man?" demanded Maggot.

"Look!"

Maggot's eyes tried to follow. He didn't see anything.

"What the hell you seein', dude?" he asked irritably.

"There, man, there!" Mikey's voice had a note of panic in it. "Over there, by the counter. It's the same bitch!"

Heedless of his facial contusions, Maggot wrinkled his forehead. He didn't see anybody. Jesus, he thought. Mikey's about strung out for sure. Guy's gonna blow his cork any minute.

Then he saw her, too. A cold knot grew in his stomach, and for the first time, he was concerned. Mikey was right on; it *was* the same bitch.

"Holy shit," he breathed. "Holy, fucking shit." Maggot reached over and took his friend's arm. He didn't know what to do. But one thing was certain; he had to find out who she was working for, and what they were doing.

But first things first, and the first thing was to get out of sight. "Come on, man," he growled at Mikey. "Let's haul ass."

Mikey didn't move. Maggot repeated the command, and Mikey finally allowed himself to be pulled in a stiff-legged walk toward a large pillar.

MARGIE WAS AS FRUSTRATED as she could ever remember being. Why should it be so difficult for the goddamn airline to find her baggage? After all, it was only three items, all properly labeled on the outside....

The person at the counter yesterday, who wasn't the person she was talking to now, had said the flight went on to Washington, D.C., Dulles to be exact.

"We'll short-stop 'em in D.C., and put 'em on the next flight back here," he had said. "Sorry for the inconvenience, ma'am."

Only they hadn't short-stopped 'em, or if they had, they had botched the throw back to New Orleans. And, to make matters worse, the young man she talked to yesterday wasn't here today. Instead, it was a young woman, new on the job and probably not too swift to begin with, and she couldn't even find any record that the bags had been lost.

Frustration ebbed through Margaret like a poison. She tried taking a slow, deep breath, angry at her own anger.

Calm down, woman, she said to herself. Be cool. You're a clinical psychologist. You counsel other people how to handle the stresses of life. You know how unproductive it is to let these things get to you. Besides, it's a blankety-blank waste of energy. Save it for the enemy, as Carl would probably say.

Jesus, she thought, did I really think that? I'll never see the guy again, I disapprove of everything he stands for, and here I am, thinking like he does?

No, she corrected herself, I don't disapprove of what he stands for. I just don't agree with his methods of getting there.

But, "save it for the enemy"? I must be going nuts.

The girl behind the counter was obviously overwhelmed by the problem. "Um, what was the flight again?" It was the third time she had asked.

"Eight twenty-three," Margie answered. "From San Francisco. Arrived here at 5:48. The young man yesterday said it was going on to Washington, D.C., Dulles."

"Do you know where it was going on to from here?"

Margie stared at her with a peculiar combination of pity and disgust. Overdeveloped mammarily—was that a word, she wondered—and underdeveloped mentally. For God's sake, girl, where's your pride? Still, society had probably made her that way. Things being the way they were, the girl probably found it easier to slide by on her smile and her boobs than to learn even the fundamentals of cognitive reasoning.

If tits were brains, she'd be the Einstein of the eighties.

Where did I ever pick that up, she wondered.

Oh, no, not Carl again. Chauvinist bastard that he was he was still generally pretty careful about how he talked around women. But sometimes he would utter those kind of crudities. Usually it was for the shock effect, like a little kid.

Bastard! I hate him. No, I love him . . . Oh, Christ, I don't know anything, anymore.

"I said, Washington, D.C.," she snapped.

The girl blinked, taken aback. "You don't have to get upset. I thought you said something about Dallas, that's all."

Margaret sighed. "Dulles. I said Dulles, not Dallas. Dulles is the name of the main airport in Washington, D.C. They don't call it Washington, D.C. International. They call it Dulles. It's named after Allen Dulles. He used to be— Oh, never mind."

With a sigh, Margaret reached across the counter and picked up a notepad with the emblem of United Airlines across the top. Resignedly she wrote, "United Flight 823, S.F. to New Or., then on to Dulles. Missing luggage: 3 pcs. American Tourister, brown." Then, as an afterthought, she added the date, then handed the slip to the young woman.

In a softer voice, she said, "Sorry I was rude. Maybe you could check around and see if anybody knows about this."

The girl looked up from the notepaper, then gave what she undoubtedly regarded as her very special smile. "Sure. No problem. Man trouble, I betcha."

"What?" Margaret's face wrinkled in bewilderment.

"Problems with your guy," the girl explained. "Don't worry, I know what it's like. I'll check on this right away." Her mission defined, happy to have a specific task, she skipped off to try to find somebody, anybody, to ask about the luggage. "Dulles, not Dallas," she repeated to herself as she left.

If tits were brains, Margaret started to think. No, she corrected herself, that's not fair. We're all sisters under the skin. Besides, maybe the little twit is more than half-right, maybe it *is* man trouble. At least, in part.

Margaret turned around and leaned her back against the counter. Idly she scanned the crowded baggage-claim area and the people from another United flight who were starting to cluster around the carousel. She glanced at the digital display that announced the flight number. By coincidence it was 823, the same flight she had taken yesterday.

She started to turn back to the counter. Something nagged at her subconscious, something about the crowd. It was something she had *looked at* but not *seen*. Christ, where did I ever pick that expression up, she wondered. Don't tell me it's another Lyonsism. It sounded like one.

She turned back and scanned the crowd. And froze as two faces leaped out in sharp focus.

The two outlaw bikers from the winery yesterday!

For an instant, her brain refused to accept the data. It can't be! Her mind whirled. How could they be here? The plane, of course, idiot, she answered herself, the same way you came. But *why* would they be here?

She stared, trying to make sure. No mistake about it, they were the ones.

The tall pallid man and the filthy, disgusting shorter one. One named Mike—no, Mikey, and the other called something else, some nickname that went with his appearance. Troll? Toad? No, that wasn't it. For some reason she thought, Larva, but that couldn't be it either, these guys wouldn't know what a larva was.

The taller one, Mikey, was staring at her. Even as she watched, the squatty one's eyes met hers, and he grabbed Mikey and tried to drag him out of sight.

Margaret turned quickly back to the counter. The girl with the buxom chest was bustling back, a look of triumph on her face. But at this point, Margaret couldn't care less about her three pieces of luggage.

There was only one thing to do. Call the Stony Man number.

A stubborn part of her mind resisted, saying that if she called Lyons so soon it would look as if she couldn't bear to be without him. But a stronger, more enduring part of her mind prevailed. Two outlaw bikers from California just happening to choose New Orleans of all places?

It's not that I'm not afraid, she thought firmly. But something's up. No way this can be coincidence. It has to be part of some secret-squirrel operation Lyons is involved in.

Damn him, damn him, damn him.

## 6

Some eighty miles from Washington, D.C., Hal Brognola, chief of operations at Stony Man Farm, stared thoughtfully at the telephone as Margaret Williams ended the call and broke the connection. He had just hung up the receiver and now sat bolt upright in a metal swivel chair, his arms folded across his chest.

He had to think this out. Something had to be done; the question was what.

Brognola was sitting in the communications room of the three-story house that served as headquarters for the Stony Man operation. The com-center, as it was sometimes called, was on the northwest corner of the first floor, adjacent to the computer room.

An oak door joined the two rooms. From the computer room, Aaron "the Bear" Kurtzman watched silently. His nickname seemed particularly appropriate at that moment: he was slumped in a chair in a burly lump, looking like Smoky just awakened from winter hibernation.

Kurtzman had initially taken the call.

It had come in on the "unrestricted line." That term was a misnomer. Strictly speaking, there was no unrestricted number for Stony Man Farm—one didn't just look up the number in the telephone book. But, in Mack Bolan's mind, a lot of things were relative, including phone access.

Some numbers were known only to selected members of the Stony Man operation. Sometimes a number would be obtained or activated for one specific mission, and only the men involved in that particular caper would know it. Other numbers were less secret, known, perhaps, by three or four operatives.

The unrestricted line was the least secret of all. As a matter of policy, it was the number that any of the Stony Man agents could give to trusted outsiders who might have to, or want to, relay a message or get in touch.

That was the number that Carl Lyons had given to Margaret in case she needed to reach him.

Kurtzman himself had originally developed the idea of multiple numbers. As Stony Man's computer expert and keeper of the sacred scrolls—in this case, maintained in the form of seemingly limitless electronic data banks—communications were his bag.

When he first proposed the phone scheme, a couple of people objected to it. It seemed too, well, just too *simple*. The Bear had responded that usually, the fewer moving parts, the better; in other words, simple was good.

"We'll have other systems, of course," he added. "But this is a good, reliable way of allowing access but controlling it."

"What does that mean?" somebody asked.

The Bear shook his head tolerantly at these electronics savages. "It will allow people who may legitimately want to reach someone here to do so without our taking an ad in the yellow pages," he explained patiently.

Rosario Blancanales, one of the three men on Able Team, was present. Always quick with a quip, he found the Bear's statement too good to pass up.

"I wonder what we'd be listed under, if we were in the book," he mused out loud. "The *F*'s? For 'Farms,' as in Stony Man Farm? Or the *A*'s, for 'Agricultural Cooperatives,' maybe? Or 'Assassins,'" he added as a rueful afterthought.

"*C* for 'Commandos'?" somebody else suggested. "Or 'Crazy,' may be more like it."

It was the usually sardonic Lyons who had capped it. "*P,*" he announced.

The others looked at him, bewildered.

"*P*, as in 'Pest Control.' You know, exterminators. We'll rid your house of whatever pests are bugging you—no pun intended. This week's special is antiterrorist spray. A single treatment keeps them down for weeks."

"Yeah, well, anyway," interrupted Kurtzman rolling his eyes in mock exasperation, "let's give it a try. Just keep in mind that even the unrestricted number isn't for mass distribution. In other words, don't be giving it out to every cute little fox you meet in some goddamn bar and would like to poke."

"What he's saying," put in Lyons sarcastically, "is let access to the number be decided by the big head, not the little one. Got it?"

All eyes turned to Blancanales.

The gregarious, popular former Green Beret put on a hurt look. "Don't be lookin' at me, man," he said with elaborately feigned innocence.

Ultimately, the system went into operation. As with just about everything he did, the Bear was right. The scheme worked, and on this summer day, he just happened to be there when Margaret's call came in. He immediately flagged it to Brognola, and as a matter of routine, taped the entire conversation. And, once he learned who the caller was or claimed to be, he called up Margaret's name on the Stony Man computers to review what they had on her.

It was not merely a matter of idle curiosity or some gratuitous breach of privacy that he did so.

From his own computerlike memory, the Bear knew that Lyons was acquainted with a Margaret Williams. He also recalled that they had been lovers years ago, before the Ironman came on board at Stony Man. He even remembered that she had been involved recently in an Able Team operation after her brother, an L.A. policeman, had been gunned down. But he didn't trust even his own amazing memory with more details than that, so he called up her name from the data banks.

Once the file was called up, Brognola could scan the information as he talked or listened. A separate CRT was installed in the communications room for just such a purpose.

Brognola could refer to an incident mentioned in the file that only a few people would know about. His purpose would be to verify that the caller was, indeed, Margaret Williams. He knew that no profile based on external investigation was ever really complete; some details of a person's life were invariably missed in even the most exhaustive background investigation.

By working through the small details, Brognola might, sooner or later, happen on an incident that an imposter would not have been briefed on.

As he sat gazing at the phone after the call was over, Brognola was satisfied of two things.

One, the caller was not an imposter.

Two, Margaret Williams was in danger.

Brognola had an instinct for those things. As Bolan's chief executive officer at Stony Man, he brought with him strategic skills developed over years with the Justice Department's covert operations group. Often, he could sense the dynamics of a mission even before enough intelligence had been gathered to form a working model of who was after whom, or why.

Today, that sense told him Margaret wasn't safe. Ironically, however, even though she was frightened, she'd refused to accept his evaluation of how much risk she was really exposed to.

"Listen, Margaret—is it okay if I call you Margaret?" he had asked only minutes before.

"Of course."

"Listen, Margaret. We don't have anything going on that bunch, but I'm still concerned."

"Or you don't want to tell me," she cut in. Irritation showed in her voice.

He shook his head, forgetting she couldn't see him. "No, that's not it. I'd tell you if we had something like that going. It's just that..."

"So there's nothing to worry about," she interrupted.

"No," he began, but she cut him off again.

"If you don't have some big, secret operation on these guys, then it's got to be a simple coincidence, right? And if it's coincidence, then there's no danger. Nothing to worry about, right?"

"Look, Margaret," the Stony Man operations chief said patiently. "That's *not* right. It's dead wrong, in fact." Even as he spoke, Brognola cringed—why did

he have to pick *that* figure of speech at this particular
time.

"Why not?" she demanded.

"First, it sometimes happens that missions are un-
dertaken before I know about them." It sometimes
happens, all right, but I'll have somebody's balls if
that's what's happening right now, he thought. "Besides, there's always the possibility that these guys
mean some harm to you because they're, uh,—" don't
say *pissed off*, he thought "—angry at Lyons over the
business at the winery."

Margaret considered that possibility and rejected it.
"That doesn't make sense. Why would they come after me because of what Carl did?"

Brognola frowned. Where had this sheltered little
girl been? "Well, for one thing, they might use you to
get back at him. For another, you would be— It would
be easier to get you than it would be to get him."

She thought that over. It made sense. Still she
couldn't shake the feeling they were holding out on
her. Them and their little commando games. Sure, the
bikers scared her, but anger and pride were at work as
well.

"No," she said abruptly. "I don't really think it's a
big deal. Really. I just wanted to pass it on to you. In
case it made any difference to whatever you were
doing."

The tone of her voice said she was about to termi-
nate the call. Brognola spoke urgently.

"Look, Margaret. The airport has a security force.
Would you mind just going over there and waiting for
a little while so I can do some checking?"

"What'll I tell them? That I date—used to date—a
guy who's a big secret agent, and a couple of bogey-

men are after me, and will you big, brave cops protect me?'' She gave a short laugh, surprised at her own bitterness. ''No way. Thanks just the same.''

''Don't worry about that. I'll call them and they'll expect you. I'll have somebody local, some big shot they'll listen to and won't question, contact them. I can also have somebody we trust in that area do some checking around.'' And maybe, he thought, I can find out if that goddamn hothead Lyons has started some kind of war we don't know about yet.

Margaret's voice became very formal and distant. ''No. No, that won't be necessary. Thank you very much, Mr. Brognola. If I see anything that looks dangerous, I'll call, never fear. Thank you for your time.''

She broke the connection.

After a while, Brognola stopped staring at the telephone. He looked over at Kurtzman and sighed.

The Bear raised an inquiring eyebrow. ''Well?''

Brognola shook his head. ''I don't know. What do you think?''

Kurtzman grinned. ''I think Lyons isn't going to be getting any off her for a while. That is one pissed-off lady.'' Then he turned serious. ''We *don't* have anything going on with these guys,'' he confirmed. ''But I think you're right—she is in danger.''

The Stony Man operations chief thought for a few moments more. Then he issued a stream of directions.

''Get somebody down in New Orleans on these guys, Maggot and Mikey, whoever the hell they are. Post haste, right now. And start checking out their backgrounds. You can probably get their last names off the airline flight information.''

"Thanks for the tip, boss," said the Bear facetiously. He knew better than anybody how to go about finding that sort of thing. His computers could access the airline manifests and turn up information that wouldn't be given to the cops without a court order.

"Sorry. Didn't meant to tell you your business," Brognola said with a grin. "Find out if there's any police report on the incident at the winery—actually, probably be a sheriff's report up in that area. If there is, get it. If there isn't, have somebody we trust talk to the guy who runs the place. Ditto on the judge these guys were rousting when our friend Lyons the diplomat intervened."

"Anything else?"

"Yeah. Do we know where Lyons is?"

"Negative." The Bear shook his head. "He usually checks in from time to time, but he was off for a couple more weeks. Officially, that is. Your orders, I recall."

Brognola nodded. "Yeah. He needed the rest. He was showing definite signs of being strung out." He gestured at the CRT screen that had Margie's file displayed on it. When he spoke, concern was evident in his voice. "According to the file, this woman and Lyons were real close. Engaged to be married, even, way back when. Broke up, got back together not long ago, and now it sounds like they're broken up again."

Kurtzman didn't comment. He knew what Brognola was driving at.

"But even if they're not speaking to each other now, it's pretty clear that Lyons loves her or used to."

"I'll buy 'used to,' I think," said Kurtzman.

"Yeah, that's probably it. But 'used to' is some-times about as bad as 'is,' when love is involved. Especially if you add guilt and anger to it.

The Bear nodded.

Brognola continued. "What I'm saying is that it doesn't matter if we had an operation going on these guys or not. If these dirt bags do something to her, for whatever reason..."

"Yeah, I know. It won't be healthy to be an outlaw biker for a while, that's for sure."

"It'll be payback city. Vengeance to the max. A bloodbath, with our boy Lyons working the faucets." Brognola's face was grim. "Bear?"

"Yes, boss?"

"Get our man in New Orleans onto Margaret. Pro-tect her. For God's sake, don't let a hair on her stub-born little head get hurt."

He paused.

"Anything else?"

"Yes. Find Lyons."

"Yes, boss."

"Find him now. And let me talk to him when you do."

The Stony Man director turned on his heel and strode from the room.

## 7

Mike Armstrong represented the best of the old school of FBI agents. That meant he was tough, tenacious and thorough. And he got results.

Even if he was an old guy.

He had retired from the Bureau six years earlier. At the time, though he wouldn't admit it to anyone, the prospect of retirement had terrified him. It was the only thing he had been afraid of in twenty years.

To Mike, being a good cop was an attitude more than anything else. It was an outlook, a way of seeing life. City policeman, federal agent, deputy sheriff— the bureaucratic distinctions were artificial and meaningless. Each group had its good cops; each had some that weren't. And all the good ones had one thing in common: they saw life as an endless fabric of mystery, of secret purpose and hidden act.

How the hell can a good investigator ever retire, he had wondered. How can you stop looking at things the way you have for the past twenty-five years? You might as well die.

No wonder so many cops ate their guns or crawled into a bottle when retirement loomed. Some ways of death were just quicker than others, that was all.

Mike, however, had done none of those things.

With the same sardonic toughness that had served him for so many years, Mike had carried on. He got a private investigator's license and had some business cards printed up. He weathered the retirement parties and the well-wishing, the dreary rituals in which the Bureau shook his hand, gave him his pension and revoked his clearances.

Within a month, Mike realized that nothing had changed. If he was surprised, he didn't show it.

The scams, the conspiracies, the hustles and the angles—they were still there. Moreover, he still had what it took. And now, five years later, he was busier than he had ever been.

Mike Armstrong was Hal Brognola's trusted man in New Orleans.

The call from Stony Man Farm came in as he and Sarah, his wife of twenty-four years, were sitting down to a dinner of chilled seafood salad. Mike opened a fresh steno pad from the supply he kept by the telephone and, as he listened, jotted notes in his own system of shorthand. When the call was over, he shut the pad and returned to the table.

Sarah looked at him. "Work, dear?"

He shrugged. "Just a little something I've been asked to check out."

"Want me to save your dinner until later?"

He shook his head. "No. This looks too good to miss. Let's eat now. If you don't mind, I'll just not take as long to enjoy it as I might have otherwise."

The dialogue had been refined over the years of their very good marriage. Mike always pretended that the work could wait on whatever meal his wife had prepared. Sarah, however, knew that from the moment Mike answered the telephone, his mind would be on whatever problem he was being asked to solve. Just as he invariably assured her there was no hurry, she always rejoined by shooing him through the meal and into action.

So, ten minutes later, Mike set his pale straw Stetson hat on his tanned pate. He kissed his wife's cheek—it was soft and somehow all the more lovely from the aging they had shared—and let himself out the door into the sultry New Orleans evening.

As it turned out, he was too late to do what Stony Man had wanted him to do.

The ten minutes for dinner hadn't mattered; it was already too late when he got the call. The ship had sailed, a fait accompli. So he dropped back and gathered what information he could, and within an hour he was on the telephone to Stony Man Farm again, making his preliminary report.

BROGNOLA AND THE BEAR listened in silence. Behind them, big silvery reels turned slowly as the recorders automatically taped the conversation for later transcription.

Mike Armstrong spoke in short, almost terse sentences.

"She caught a cab outside the terminal right after she talked to you. An independent, Mercury Cabs. The driver radioed he was in service at 7:23."

"Go on," Brognola urged.

"The cab was found at 8:35. It had apparently been forced off the road a few miles north of the airport. The driver's body was in the trunk. Stabbed, throat cut. Been dead about an hour, which fits with the distance from the airport. Whoever took them out didn't waste much time at it."

"What about the woman?"

"Gone. No sign of her."

"How sure are you that she was the passenger? That this was the cab she got into?"

"Pretty damn sure. Girl at the customer assistance desk for Delta saw her walk right out and get into a blue cab. Mercury's are blue, and its a small company, so there aren't many of them. Plus the timing fits."

"Anything else?"

"Yes. The homicide crew is processing the cab right now. They're playing it close to the vest, as usual, but I was able to find out that it looks like the interior was wiped clean. No prints."

"So," the Stony Man operations chief mused, "they sure didn't waste any time. Anything else?"

"Not at this point. Cab shows some red paint transfers on it, on the driver's side. Could be from whatever vehicle forced it off the road, or it could be from an earlier sideswipe. They're looking into it, though."

Mike finished speaking and waited. The silence lasted most of a minute. All three men knew that any chance of using the red paint transfer was remote at best. Even assuming it came from the attacker's vehicle, its value as evidence depended on getting a lead on who the assailants were, then seeing if it matched any car or truck they had access to.

In other words, the paint could be good courtroom evidence to confirm or deny that a certain vehicle had been involved. But they still had to come up with a suspect vehicle before the tests could be made.

"Not much to go on," said Brognola at last.

"Yeah," agreed Mike. "It's probably a dead end. For now, anyway."

"Unless?" prompted Brognola.

The former FBI agent shrugged, forgetting the others couldn't seem him. "My guess is there are only two ways this case is likely to be broken at this point."

"And those are?"

"One, a chance witness."

"Like what?"

"Somebody accidentally saw what happened and hasn't reported it yet."

Brognola thought for a moment. "I'll play devil's advocate to your theory, Mike. Why wouldn't the guy report it when he saw it?"

"Maybe the guy didn't want to get involved. Maybe he had some unpaid parking tickets, and he thought he would get arrested if he talked to the cops. Maybe he's a married guy who was with some female person not his wife. Whatever it is, we could luck out like that."

"And the other way?" Both Brognola and Kurtzman knew what the answer would be.

Mike spoke deliberately. "These guys Maggot and Mikey. They're the link at this point. If I were the cops, and I knew about these guys, I'd be looking for them and their friends and associates, fellow bikers—whatever. I'd keep widening the circle until I came up with a red car or truck."

Brognola didn't respond. Mike let the unasked question hover between them. Finally the Stony Man chief answered it.

"No," he said at last. "No, I don't think we're in a position to disclose the information about Maggot and Mikey to the police just yet."

Mike listened in silence. A lifetime of involvement in sensitive cases served him well at this point. The brass would tell him what they felt he needed to know. Presumably they saw the big picture. If they didn't want to give the local cops information that would help the investigation, there was a reason for it. Mike was used to that, and he accepted it. They called the plays; he ran them as best he could.

"No," Brognola continued, as if agreeing with himself. "In fact, I think we'll conduct our own, uh, investigative efforts first."

"Anything more from my end?" inquired Mike.

"There may be later. Meantime, just keep following whatever the cops have going."

They ended the call. Brognola turned to the Bear. "You ever get a lead on Lyons?"

"Negative."

"Keep trying."

"Roger."

The Stony Man chief thought for a few moments. "You know," he said finally, "this has the smell of something more than a private vendetta. Something's going down here, and I have a hunch we'll be involved in it."

"How so, boss?"

"I don't know. As I said, it's just a hunch. It might not be a bad idea if you checked out if anything's going on in Louisiana."

"You want me to check San Francisco, too? The wine country?"

Brognola shook his head. "No, not yet, anyway. My gut says it's New Orleans. Let's start there. Why don't you fire up those fancy machines of yours and start gathering whatever sounds promising? Shake the trees a little, and let's see what falls out.''

Kurtzman grinned. This was his kind of work. "You got it, boss. You want a rundown on all crime committed in the last forty-eight hours in Cajun country, no sweat. Anything bigger than a shoplifting, we'll get it.''

## 8

It was three o'clock in the morning when Kurtzman's machines came through with a possible answer.

He scanned the screen. This had to be it.

The Stony Man computers could access virtually every form of electronic communication in the country. Microwaves, satellite transmissions, radio—anything could be intercepted if you knew where to look. And, it amused Kurtzman to admit, if you didn't worry about doing a few things that technically amounted to committing about a dozen separate felonies.

The Bear knew where to look. Moreover, he didn't mind committing a few felonies here and there. All in the line of duty, so to speak.

The privacy laws he was technically violating amused him.

Any sophisticated spying operation with the bucks to get the hardware could do what he was doing. Moreover, he knew that they did. It went on all the time.

The crowning irony was that the only ones who generally couldn't access this information were the legitimate law-enforcement agencies of the government. This, he knew, was due largely to the pressure of self-proclaimed protectors of the constitution, the misguided civil libertarians who created the specter of big brother listening in on every intimate call between a clerk-typist at a bank and her boyfriend on a job site somewhere.

He shook his head ruefully.

As if we, that is the government, would have the time or resources to undertake that kind of wholesale monitoring. Or would want to, for God's sake.

Yet, laws were passed making it so difficult to legally access such information that organized crime and subversive activities of all sorts flourished, unchecked by traditional law-enforcement efforts. The bad guys not only could and did listen in—illegally, of course—but they were protected from any effective prosecution by the same privacy laws they were violating.

Of course, building a legal case for prosecution was the farthest thing from Kurtzman's mind at the moment.

"So what's a few felonies between friends?"

There was nobody else in the room when the Bear spoke. In the manner of a true genius, he frequently thought out loud. When he did so, he talked to himself in his normal voice, even though he was alone in the room. Of course, in some respects that was preferable to talking out loud to himself when there *was* somebody else in the room. Listening to the one-sided conversations of Stony Man's lumpy electronics genius could be unnerving.

Where to begin, he wondered.

As with more conventional detective activities, there was a lot of legwork involved in gathering the information he was after. He had to figure out what was significant and why. He had to sort through all the millions of pieces of information being transmitted and find the incidents that looked promising.

It was grunt work, but it was necessary. Instead of pounding the pavement, though, he pounded the keyboard of the massive electronic monsters he had installed and programmed.

So Kurtzman put his brilliant mind to doing what logical analysis is all about.

Simplifying.

Kurtzman knew that genius meant being able to see the big picture.

That meant he couldn't be distracted by all the irrelevant data. He had to focus on and isolate the basic factors at work. He had to find the why beneath the what. It was just what Isaac Newton had done when he looked at all the physical phenomena of falling bodies, the whats, and had then been able to deduce the law of gravity, the why.

The Bear put his genius to work.

As he saw it, there were three possibilities.

One, Margaret had been taken by random attackers to be raped, robbed or killed as were thousands of other Americans every year. Two, she and Lyons had known about something involving these people and she had been kidnapped so that she could be silenced. Three—which the Bear realized was merely a variation of the second hypothesis—her attackers had been up to something that they *thought* she knew about, and she had been attacked because of that.

The idea of a random attack, a couple of subhumans falling on somebody who looked like a good subject for whatever they wanted to do, didn't seem likely. True, thought the Bear, it happened all the time, thanks in large part to the inefficiencies of the courts in protecting the public from criminals. But it would be a hell of a coincidence for it to happen to her at this particular time.

"Coincidences happen, Aaron, me boy," he said aloud to himself as he slumped before the computer console, arms folded across his chest.

"Even to folks like us?" he asked.

"Even to us," he answered himself. "Just because we're the special executives of the world's most powerful government doesn't mean we can control everything."

"We could be struck by lightning, too, just like anybody else," he added.

Still, a random attack didn't sound right, didn't have the right feel. Why would these two goons follow her from San Francisco to New Orleans just to casually attack her? And, according to what she had told Brognola on the telephone, they had panicked when she saw them.

Of course, they could have followed her to take revenge for what Lyons had done up at the winery. But even that didn't add up—they would have to have a hell of a grudge to follow her that far. Besides, how would they even know they would be able to find her a day later in New Orleans?

Kurtzman respected Brognola's judgment on matters like this, and the Stony Man operations chief had felt the same way. How had he put it? Something about how it smelled like more than a private vendetta? "Something's going down here, and I just have a hunch we'll be involved in it," he added.

Again Kurtzman spoke to himself out loud. "All right, Aaron, me boy, so where are we? If it wasn't a random attack or a private vendetta, what was it? Make your hypothesis. Take your best shot.''

He assumed that something had gone down, that an incident had happened that was tied to Margaret's kidnapping and, though he didn't like to admit it, to her murder probably. It was likely that she was dead by this time. There had to be something out there that she knew about or, more precisely, that her attackers *thought* she knew about that made it worth their taking the risk of murdering a cab driver to get at her.

Was it something Lyons had been working on when they were together?

Strictly speaking, it shouldn't have been.

The Stony Man project, as created by Mack Bolan and now run largely by Hal Brognola, didn't as a rule have to go looking for business. The projects came to them, usually directly or indirectly from the White House. When all else failed, Bolan's boys were the ultimate messy projects squad, the last resort of the President, or some other high-ranking executive officer.

Still the secret agent didn't exist who wasn't always looking and listening, testing the wind, keeping his eyes open for something he might end up involved in. The motive wasn't to generate business, exactly, but to know what was going on.

The Bear knew. He played the same game himself.

And it wasn't too uncommon that he could read a newspaper story—reading what *wasn't* in the story as well as what was—and predict that some affiliated job was going to drop into their laps from the Oval Office.

All agents did it. Whether they did it because they were agents or they did it by natural inclination, guys who were good at it were the ones who didn't get their asses shot off. It was a fact of life.

And Carl Lyons, the aggressive and inquisitive ex-cop, was the worst of the lot. He was most inclined to stick his nose where it hadn't yet been ordered by Brognola.

"All of which means that something is probably up, and either Margaret knew about it, or the bad guys thought she did, and they took her out."

As he thought it over and said it out loud, the Bear knew—he felt—that had to be it.

To find out what was up, he had to start looking and listening, through his computers, to what was going on in Louisiana. Something had happened, something big enough to warrant kidnapping and murder—one killing for sure and probably two. Something bigger than a shoplifting, as he had put it to Brognola.

It was a problem of narrowing it down.

So the Bear wrote a computer program to do just that.

It was a seat-of-the-pants affair that was designed to focus on those elements that would be present in any communication that was serious enough to be what he was looking for.

The program required a combination of logic, guesswork and hunch. As the evening progressed, he refined it, adding some factors and deleting others, but the principle remained the same. Essentially, the program scanned the data for anything secret or top secret, anything designated by the sender as highly urgent or top priority and anything that might involve the military or that was directed to certain sensitive agencies.

By 2:00 a.m., he had noticed a series of highly urgent communications from Louisiana involving the Nuclear Regulatory Commission.

That looked promising.

By 2:20, it was clear the FBI was involved. That looked even more interesting.

By 2:50, the Bear had tapped into a top-secret conversation about a large quantity of nuclear waste that was missing from a disposal sight near New Orleans. He'd learned that there were no suspects at that time but that investigators were theorizing that a white-supremacy group was behind it.

The Bear clicked over into brainstorm mode.

Hijacked nuclear waste—that didn't happen every day. The suspects were believed to be some Aryan power group, for reasons he didn't know yet.

Outlaw bikers were frequently white-supremist types, he knew. Ties between members of the Hell's Angels and the Aryan Brotherhood prison gang were already documented. Maggot and Mikey, the prime suspects in the kidnapping and murder, were both outlaw bikers, members of a club known for its sympathy for such views.

White supremists, outlaw bikers, missing nuclear waste—it was starting to add up.

"That's it," the Bear said aloud, alone in the computer room. "It has to be."

Kurtzman realized, of course, that there was a lot he didn't know. He still didn't know any of the whys, for instance. Why kidnap Margie? What was her link to the nuclear waste? Had she just happened into this by accident? Did it involve something Lyons was mixed up in? And, the biggest why of all—why had the nuclear waste been hijacked in the first place?

As he looked at it, he realized there were more questions than answers. But questions were a good start, and instinct told him this was the real thing.

He reached for the com line and buzzed Brognola's quarters. Time to rouse the boss.

THE STONY MAN operations chief listened in silence to Kurtzman's report. When the Bear finished, Brognola asked a single question.

"Have we received anything official on this?"

Kurtzman shook his head. "Not that I'm aware of. Why? Are you expecting something?"

Brognola hedged. "It's nothing specific, really. This just has the feel of something we might get pulled in on. Depending on what these wackos want with the hot stuff, the isotopes, there may not be time to investigate and arrest in accordance with, uh, Supreme Court formalities."

The Bear looked closely at his chief. This was the second time that Brognola had hinted at Stony Man's involvement in whatever was going on.

Could it be that Brognola had already been advised that something like this might be coming down? Did somebody, somewhere, the President, for instance, have some advance intelligence that had already been passed on to Brognola. Was Stony Man on standby alert, even before Margaret's call?

Brognola's face gave no clue. One thing was certain: the Stony Man chief would tell him when and if he was supposed to know.

Still, Kurtzman decided to needle his boss a little.

"Without Supreme Court formalities?" he repeated.

Brognola nodded.

"And that means...?" continued the Bear.

Brognola looked at him. "That means us."

## 9

Gunfire ripped through the early-morning coolness.

Flat on his back, shielded by an outcropping of rock, Rosario Blancanales watched the puffs of dirt as the bullets stitched a line above and a few yards off to one side of him along the embankment he hid behind.

Autoburn, he thought. Hot fire, as opposed to slow fire.

That meant the weapon was being fired in the full-automatic mode. A man pulled the trigger once, and the rifle would keep firing by itself until he released the trigger or the ammo was used up or the damned thing jammed or overheated.

He waited, muscles tense, mind alert and ready.

Adrenaline surged through him. Then, suddenly, the autoburn came to an abrupt halt. The trained ear—and his was trained—could pick up the distinctive *clack* of the receiver locking open an instant after the sound of a rifle's last shot. That meant the ammo was gone. Clip used up. Gun empty, waiting for the operator to twist out the dry magazine and clap in a fresh one.

It was his cue, and he was ready for it.

"Now!" The mind screamed the order to the body, the instant the gunfire stopped, and he was on his feet, running like hell across the field of fire, sprinting for the eight-foot wall forty yards ahead.

At any moment, the gunfire would begin again.

He wore black athletic shoes, black trousers and a green-and-brown camouflage shirt. A nylon shoulder rig held a .45 Government Model under his left armpit; his main weapon was an M-16, the workhorse military combat rifle in .223 caliber.

Feet alternately gripping, then pushing off with the explosive power of a strong, quick man in peak condition, Blancanales arrowed for the wall.

It was made of railroad ties—solid, impenetrable. And high. His first task was to get there and over it, preferably without undergoing any modifications to his body structure. Lead poisoning kills, as they say.

The ground rushed by. Then the wall loomed before him, and, in a single motion, Blancanales leaped.

Grabbing for a hold with one hand, he added the pull of his arm to the upward momentum of the jump. Then he was on the top, going over on his belly, lying parallel to the top of the wall. *Never silhouette yourself!* Christ, they had drilled that into him, beginning at boot camp and continuing through a dozen other more specialized—and less known—schools paid for courtesy of Uncle Sam.

He dropped down on the far side, legs buckling to absorb the impact as he hit the ground. Then he rolled to his feet, already in motion.

Some ten yards ahead was the house.

It was just where Kissinger had said it would be, and Blancanales sprinted for it. There was no time for subtlety. He headed straight for the front door, ready to burst in and hose the room with the M-16, taking them all out, friend or foe, never mind which was which, and sort the bodies out later....

Nicknamed "the Politician," or simply "Pol," Blancanales had in one sense been trained his whole life for endeavors such as this.

The son of Mexican nationals, he had grown up in the barrios of Los Angeles and San Ysidro, the latter a border community between San Diego on the American side and Tijuana on the Mexican side. As a skinny brown kid, he and his five brothers and sisters had worked and played in the streets and in their parents' Mexican restaurant.

Today, at forty or thereabouts—*más o menos*, as he would put it with a wink, using the Spanish phrase for "more or less"—the skinny kid was now a man, broad shouldered and solid. Startling streaks of gray ran through his jet black hair and mustache. His dark forehead was well lined, but his complexion was healthy and somehow even youthfullooking despite the lines.

Between his childhood and today, Blancanales had been forged against the anvil of war to make him what he was now, a counterterrorist expert attached to one of the most elite and secret quasiofficial groups in the world.

Stony Man Farm. To be more precise, Able Team.

Like his friend, Carl Lyons, the Politician was one of a handful of the most dangerous men alive, notwithstanding the easy manner and charm that had earned him his nickname.

In the second half of the sixties, during the height of the Vietnam war, Blancanales had enlisted in the army. Once there, he had looked around and decided it was going to be Special Forces for him.

"Why, for God's sake?" asked Pete Banfield, one of the other recruits. Pete was one of those laid-back, good-humored types, a hell of a nice guy but a natural and witty bullshit artist.

Banfield's tone was incredulous.

It was during the fourth week of boot camp, a particularly arduous spell when the DIs were pouring it to them. The recruits had been there long enough to be half-seasoned but not yet long enough to know they would actually make it through.

Blancanales had countered with the easy grin that was his trademark. "Why not?"

"Why not?" His friend looked at him, aghast. "Look at this shit we're going through. You want eight more weeks of this? Or however long it is?"

Blancanales shrugged. Banfield continued.

"Look, man, I've heard about jump school. It makes boot look like a cakewalk. They'll do their best to bust your ass. And for what? So they can put you a fucking mile up in the air and kick you out of a perfectly good airplane. Why go through all that?"

The Politician winked. "I'm afraid of heights. Might help me get over it. Besides," he added, "it's only three weeks."

His buddy shook his head. "And then, if you survive that, they'll send you to the hottest spots in Nam."

"Beats unloading produce trucks. Besides, they even give you a set of silver wings, right? And a beret? I always did like green."

Banfield rolled his eyes. "Father forgive him, for he knows not what he's fucking saying," he intoned in mock reverence. Then a terrible thought struck him. "Say, Blank, were you drafted?"

Blancanales was puzzled. "Huh?"

"Were you drafted, man?" When he received no admission or denial, Banfield continued, his voice expressing his amazement. "You *volunteered*, didn't you? You didn't get drafted. You signed up on your own. And now you're talking about volunteering for jump school?" He shook his head in mock disgust. "Man's clearly psychotic," he muttered. "Wacko. Stone-cold wacko."

The Politician grinned but didn't respond. Banfield continued his diatribe.

"Me, I got drafted. I'm here thanks to my old lady and Uncle Sam. My ex-old lady, that is."

Pol looked at him. "How'd your old lady get into the act?"

"I had one of those draft deferments. A couple of them actually. Dependents—that's what she was—plus I had a job lined up in a defense plant. Meant you got put in a lower draft category. Women and children first. That sort of thing. Suited me just fine."

"So what happened?" urged Pol, intrigued.

"She stopped being a dependent. My *de*pendent old lady became an *in*dependent ex-old lady."

"How so?"

Banfield laughed ruefully. "Got herself a new boyfriend. Left me, got a divorce. So there went that exemption."

"What about the job at the defense plant?"

"She wrote my draft board a letter and told them I didn't have any dependents anymore and that I had decided against taking the job at the defense plant. Probably figured that since the judge didn't order any alimony, she didn't have any interest in my staying alive."

"Holy *Madre de Dios*," breathed Blancanales. "'Hell hath no fury...'"

"No shit," exclaimed Banfield. "And the hell of it is I had just accepted the defense job, but by then it was too late. The draft board plucked me out, and here I am, enjoying running my ass off in the rain and knowing that when this is over, I'll get to do the same thing in rice paddies with gooks shooting at me. She's driving my ex-car, banging her new boyfriend in my ex-bed in my ex-house."

"Tough luck," observed the Politician sympathetically. Although he didn't agree with Banfield's beliefs about military service and the draft, he couldn't help but sympathize.

"And to think," Banfield continued, "you didn't even have to be here." He thought a moment, then brightened. "On the other hand, in some ways this is better than being with my old lady. Not worse, anyway."

Blancanales grinned and shook his head without reply.

"At least it's only for two years," Banfield continued. "Or less, if I get my ass blown away."

Despite his wisecracks about conquering his fear of heights and getting a pretty green beret, Blancanales had good reasons for wanting jump school. They were the same reasons that later led him to go to jungle warfare school and still later to take on missions that nobody else wanted. They were reasons he wasn't sure he could explain, even though he understood them himself.

It had to do with duty. Principle. Doing what ought to be done.

He believed with complete conviction in what America stood for, even though under its laws his own parents were considered to be criminals—illegals, wetbacks. And what America stood for, to his way of thinking, was freedom and opportunity—things worth giving something back to his country for in order to preserve them.

There was something else involved as well, a special ingredient that only fighting men know.

Defining it wasn't easy.

It involved friendship but was more than that. It was akin to loyalty but was more than that, also. It was a special selflessness that combined honor, duty, pride and probably a couple of other things as well. It was what made men throw themselves on grenades or charge flaming guns when all the choices were bad but this one might do some good for the big picture even if it meant lights out for yourself. . . .

The Politician had it instinctively.

In jump school, he had been made the stick leader, the man designated to lead his particular stick or squad. His indomitable will and refusal to be broken had formed the backbone of the stick.

He still remembered that first week and the dreaded thirty-four-foot tower. It was jump school folklore that all the candidates would have to jump off a thirty-four-foot tower. What the folklore didn't tell them— what was deliberately withheld from them, in fact— was that a special harness would stop them from hitting the ground.

When the qualifying jumps came around, jump school was almost over. The worst of the hazing was finished. The six-foot tower and the thirty-four-foot tower were history. All a candidate needed then were the qualifying jumps.

Five of them.

That meant five times a man had to hook up, first the left riser, then the right one. Five times he had to stand in the hatch of the ancient C-47, a twin-engined DC-3 made by Douglas Aircraft that was still in service at Fort Benning's jump school when Blancanales went through. Five times a man would hear the deafening roar of the engines and the rushing air and look down to see a few thousand feet of nothing.

Five times he had to wait, alone in the maelstrom of noise and energy, and five times he had to do it: step out of "a perfectly good airplane," as Banfield had put it. Then came the jump, the blast of air, then the snap-yank of the chute opening. After that, a man knew that he was committed and that nothing could stop the fact that the ground was hauling ass up at him, waiting for him to tuck, hit, bend, drop and roll.

After the fifth one, they pinned on the wings, the silver wings of the Airborne. A man got clear of his chute, hustled over and fell out for the presentation. Right there in the field. Unless he got hurt and had to go to sick bay.

For the Politician, it wasn't five jumps; it was six.

As stick leader, he kept track of each of the men in the squad and of their jumps. "Do it scared if you have to, but nut up and do it," Blancanales told his squad before the first jump. His quiet voice and ever-present wink mitigated the harshness of his words.

As the fifth round was coming up, he suddenly realized they were one man short.

He ran over the men in his mind and came up with the missing man.

"Hodges," he said aloud. "Hodges. Where the hell is he?"

None of the other men in the squad had seen the lanky youth from the Midwest. He was a solemn, slow-talking kid whose father had been a paratrooper in the Second World War and had been in the D-day invasion of Normandy. Hodges was serious and reliable and wanted more than anything in the world to be a paratrooper; it was inconceivable he would have scrubbed so close to the end of the program.

The Politician sprinted for the barracks. He bounded up the stairs and into the empty structure, eyes probing the relative gloom inside for the youth.

Nothing.

Then a strange sound reached him. It was a peculiar grunt, halfway between a gagging noise and a gasp of pain.

Blancanales had heard the stories of suicide, of nerve-shattered young men who chose death over the dishonor of being washed out. The barrack's folklore even contained a story of a soldier who'd hanged himself after his third qualifying jump, even though his record had been unblemished up to that point.

Blancanales heard the sound again.

"No!" he hissed. "No!" Hodges seemed like the last guy who would do something like that, but who could tell? His dad had parachuted at Normandy; that was a hell of a lot to live up to.

Then he saw it.

Relief flooded over him as his eyes made out the lanky farm boy sitting on his cot. His back was to Blancanales, and he was doubled over, his chest against his knees, but at least he wasn't hanging.

The Politician was there in three leaps. "Hodges!" he barked.

After a moment, the young man turned toward Blancanales. His ashen face was set in granite, marred only by a single tear. Then Blancanales looked down.

Hodges's right foot was in his paratrooper boot, which was laced and tied off. His left ankle, however, was the size of a grapefruit, and he was trying to force it into the stiff, dark leather. He choked back the pain, gagging on his own bile as he struggled.

"What happened?" asked Blancanales, though he already knew. Without waiting for a reply, he knelt and examined the ankle. It was badly broken. The shin stretched over the swelling was shiny and glistening.

"Third jump," mumbled Hodges. "I hit bad and hurt it. I can't get the boot on over it."

Blancanales looked puzzled. "I thought you did four jumps."

"I have."

The Politician stared at him. That was all the kid said. "I have." And yet, that said it all. With a broken ankle, Hodges had gotten back in line and gone up and jumped again. God and Hodges alone knew what it must have felt like to land.

That took guts, pure and simple.

Blancanales made up his mind without hesitation. It was obvious the foot wouldn't go into the boot. No way, not with that much swelling. It would be like putting ten pounds of flour in a five pound bag. "Can you make it over to sick bay?"

Hodges shook his head. "They'll scrub me," he said in a husky whisper. "I can't...my dad..." His words trailed off, and he swallowed heavily.

"Can you make it over to sick bay after your fifth jump?" the Politician repeated.

Hodges looked up at him gravely. "I don't see how I'll be able to get my boot on," he explained patiently, though it struck him as odd that his stick leader couldn't see that it was impossible. "I've tried, and there's just no way. It's just too swollen. I can take the pain, but . . ."

Blancanales grabbed Hodges by the shoulder, his powerful fingers gripping strongly. "You aren't listening to me. Listen again, very carefully." He spoke slowly, giving each word deliberate emphasis. "I said, can you make it to sick bay after your fifth jump, not can you make it after you make your fifth jump. You get my drift?"

Hodges gave him a long, searching look through narrowed eyes. Finally he started to speak.

The Politician cut him off. "Good. After your fifth jump, haul ass to sick bay. They'll give you your wings there." He reached for Hodges's helmet, which had Hodges's name and serial number taped onto it. "Hell of a note to bust up your ankle on the fifth jump, ain't it?"

Hodges said nothing. Blancanales dumped his own helmet on the cot and jammed Hodges's on in its place. He pulled it low over his eyes, strapped it into place and sprinted out of the barracks to join the line of men. As Hodges.

Both men got their silver wings that day. Both men learned a little about that special bond among fighting men.

The Politician added this special toughness to his principles of freedom and doing right. He had no way of knowing that in one sense it was all a form of training for the day he would meet Mack Bolan and embark on a way of life that began in Vietnam and continued now with Stony Man Farm.

But in another sense, Blancanales didn't regard his principles as anything special. They were what separated man from the animals.

The Politician always put his money where his mouth was. In Vietnam, that meant laying his ass on the line whenever the need arose.

Long-range recon patrols. Night jumps behind enemy lines. The Silver Star, two Purple Hearts. Mission after mission, all of them bad ones, some just worse than others. Lines developed in his young face, running across his forehead. He refined his chameleon quality, became more perceptive, more quick-witted. The Blancanales smile was always there. He could move in any circle with an easy charm that made him a natural for the position of world's best spy or world's greatest con man.

Fortunately—for him as well as for the rest of the world—he chose the former.

It was in Vietnam that he met a man named Mack Bolan.

Bolan was himself Special Forces, a sergeant at the time. Though they came from entirely different backgrounds, the men quickly saw the common elements in their beliefs, their common reasons for being there.

Blancanales remembered an early mission with Bolan. Some six hours before, the Politician had returned to the fire base from an outing that had kept him awake for forty-eight hours. He had made his report and had been racked out for four hours when he was awakened.

At the CO's tent, he saw the tall man whom at that point he knew only slightly. Bolan put formalities aside and got right to the point.

"We need a sixth man for a little detail we've got to do. You in?"

"Sure."

"How long you been without sleep?"

The Politician glanced at his watch. "About three minutes now," he replied without expression.

The acting CO, a nervous young golden-boy captain named Waldon, winced. He didn't know much about Sergeant Bolan, just that the guy was Special Forces, attached to some heavyweight, top-secret detail. In Waldon's experience, that meant that traditional notions of rank became less important, unreliable even, because even though the guy was only a sergeant, he was probably working under the direct orders of some colonel somewhere, maybe even a general.

Goddamn these secret-squirrel types, anyway, Waldon thought. He started to speak, intending to compensate for the flippancy of the Politician's response.

Bolan silenced the captain with a raised hand.

The gesture was so instinctively authoritative that Waldon's suspicions were confirmed. Hell, for that matter, the guy could *be* a colonel, traveling as a sergeant for some unknown reason related to whatever crazy mission he was on.

To Blancanales, Bolan said, "You just came out of Indian country a few hours ago. You don't have to go on this one." His voice was all business.

"I know that."

"I don't want you going to sleep on us."

"I won't go to sleep."

Bolan looked at him for several moments, then nodded. "Good. Let's get moving."

In that brief exchange and in the mission that followed, Bolan recognized a courage that rivaled his own. The two men had developed a friendship that carried them past Vietnam to Bolan's personal war against the Mafia and beyond that to the Stony Man operation, Bolan's ultimate brainchild.

From the streets of the barrios to Stony Man Farm in the mists of Virginia's Blue Ridge Mountains, the son of Mexican illegals had become, along with Hermann "Gadgets" Schwarz and Carl Lyons, one of the ultimate defenders of the American way.

Today, years later, nothing had changed. Outwardly Pol was still the same wisecracking charmer; inwardly he remained firmly committed to his principles of right, honor and duty.

He was also in the best shape he'd been in his life, thanks to a self-imposed regimen that made boot camp look like a picnic. And, as he'd arrowed for the wall, expecting the gunfire to resume at any instant, the merciless training had served him well.

Now the Politician was sprinting toward the house ahead of him. He knew what would be inside and, though there were times when a cautious or silent approach was called for, this wasn't one of them.

He bounded up the two steps to the low porch and kicked in the door.

The M-16 wasn't his weapon of choice for kicking open doors and hosing down the occupants of a room. For one thing, it was longer than he liked for room entries—for wheeling around doorjambs and that kind of thing. For another, the .223 round had so high a velocity that it tended to penetrate too many layers of wall before it stopped—not an ideal feature in an urban area where there might be friendlies or neutrals.

Still, a man used what he had and to hell with it. This wasn't golf, for God's sake. There was no caddy with an Abercrombie and Fitch bag full of weapons from which he could select the best one for each hole. "Looks like a silenced Ingram 9 mm for this one, sir. Keep an eye on the water..."

The right tool was any one that got the job done.

Blancanales burst inside, slanting to one side and firing with the M-16 clamped against his hip. He autoburned the full clip, raking the human shapes with deadly .223 firepower. Orange flames shot from the muzzle of the carbine in the gloom of the structure. The sound of the gunfire was thunderous.

As the weapon locked open, he dropped to the ground and twisted out the clip as he rolled. He discarded it and slapped in a new one, then rolled to his feet to be ready for any reprisal.

Nothing moved.

No reprisals.

His mind had recorded at least six human shapes. That would be six more souls charged to his account, six more lives to add to the balance forward column by whoever was keeping the books.

He wondered if his accounts were in heaven or in hell. It struck him there were two sets of books, one in each place.

A few moments later he heard a movement outside.

"Don't shoot, amigo!" someone shouted at him from outside. The familiar booming voice belonged to John "Cowboy" Kissinger. Then the porch creaked, a shadow fell across the doorway, and the Cowboy's face appeared. Behind him, stopwatch in hand, stood the third Able Team member, their resident mad scientist, "Gadgets" Schwarz.

Kissinger surveyed the devastation inside the room. "Holy shee-itt!" he exclaimed. "Tell you to do a job, and you damn well do it, don't you!"

"Orders is orders," quipped Blancanales with a grin. "What was my time?"

Kissinger consulted the electronic digital timer in his hand. "From the time my M-16 locked open and you started running until you stopped firing was—" he consulted the timer again "—eleven point two four. Not bad. Not bad at all. And that's going over the wall, too. Where'd you learn to run that fast, anyway?"

It was Gadgets who responded. "Probably from always being chased by the cops as a kid," he quipped. "You know how these brown types are."

"Stealing hubcaps," agreed the Politician with a grin.

"Of course," continued Kissinger, "we still don't know if you're dead or alive yet. Let's see how many of the targets you hit."

Together they examined the cardboard cutouts—the forms Blancanales had seen as he burst inside the room. They had been arranged by Kissinger, a former narcotics agent and the current weapons expert at Stony Man Farm. It was he who had devised this particular drill, installing a specially built mock-up of a house at the Stony Man Farm rifle range.

Nicknamed "Cowboy" perhaps due to his tendencies to bend rules and regulations, Kissinger had come aboard the Stony Man team following the death of Andrzej Konzaki.

Kissinger had been variously a pro football player—two seasons with the Cleveland Browns—a federal narcotics agent with the Drug Enforcement Administration and later a weapons designer and consultant with Beretta, Colt and H&K, to name a few. Tough and independent, with a practical approach to the gun business—"they're tools, for God's sake, just make sure you have the best available"—he was the ideal candidate to take over Konzaki's position.

The target Kissinger now held was clean, not a hole in it anywhere.

"Oh, well," shrugged Pol, "that's why you reload. Besides, you gotta have one to interrogate."

"Bullshit." It was Gadgets who responded. An inveterate jokester, the Able Team member winked at Kissinger. Then, taking the silhouette from Kissinger, he raised his voice and pointed at Blancanales in mock seriousness. "You're not getting off that easy. Face it, pal. You missed. This guy ain't gonna say shit, and you know it. In fact, I think you oughtta run through it again, until you get it right." He tossed the cardboard silhouette onto the floor, then turned and started moving over to the second target.

A single shot boomed inside the small room. The sound reverberated off the walls and caused Kissinger and Gadgets to leap in shock.

"Jesus!" the Cowboy exclaimed, whirling to check the source of the noise.

It was Blancanales, standing over the silhouette target. His .45 Government Model was in his right hand, and a single hole had appeared in the forehead of the target.

"What'd you do that for?" demanded Kissinger, slightly annoyed.

Blancanales shrugged, suppressing a grin. He enjoyed the fact that he had startled his hecklers.

"Hell, you said he wasn't going to talk. In that case, why not?"

They checked the rest of the targets, Kissinger muttering something about "crazy bastard" as they did so. Every one of the remaining targets had at least two ten-ring hits. One of them had four plus one in about the place where the groin would be.

"The leader of the terrorists," said Blancanales with a wink.

"I figured that," agreed Kissinger. He clapped his friend on the shoulder. "Come on, let's get back to the Farm. The pager went off while you were going through the drill. I've got the feeling something's about to break. Things have been quiet for too long."

"Wait a minute," objected Blancanales. "It's your turn to do it. Him, too, for that matter," he added, pointing at Gadgets.

"Do what?" asked Kissinger innocently.

"The course. Run, over the wall, kick the door and shoot. It's your turn," he repeated.

Kissinger shook his head. "I told you. We have to get back to Stony Man."

"Hell, I did it in under twelve seconds. That means you should be able to make it in, oh, half a minute or so. Same with Gadgets, here. We can spare one minute before we have to get moving."

"Negative, buddy."

"What do you mean, 'negative'?"

"I'm the consultant, man," he said with a grin. "The coach. The teacher. I get paid for my brains, not my brawn. And as for him—" Kissinger pointed at

Gadgets "—unlike you, he doesn't need the practice."

Blancanales shook his head. "'Those that can, do,'" he quoted. "'And those that can't, teach'... right?"

Cowboy nodded and beamed. "Right on, partner. Right on. And for what it's worth, you were an inspiration to me, son. Truly an inspiration. But—" he stopped and lit a cigar, then continued through a cloud of blue smoke "—you still ain't getting me to go over that wall."

Together, they turned and headed for the jeep.

## 10

"Nuclear waste. About five tons of it. All used up for purposes of being suitable for a reactor but still hot as hell." Brognola looked around the conference room at Stony Man Farm as he spoke.

It was an entirely different ball game now. And, as usual, Brognola's instinct had been right on.

By 5:00 a.m., Kurtzman's computers had finished spitting out the data on the heist. Three hours later, the White House had telephoned, not the President, but the secretary of state.

Just over twenty-four hours later, by ten the next morning to be exact, Able Team, including Carl Lyons, had been located and assembled in the Stony Man conference room.

It was a council of war, except that they didn't know yet exactly who the enemy was or where to find him. Brognola brought the rest of the team up to speed.

As chief of operations at Stony Man Farm, and Mack Bolan's chief liaison with the White House, Brognola had taken the secretary's call on the preceding day. Actually the call had been a relatively brief one, considering the circumstances.

"Expect a courier with a complete set of the reports by 0600 hours," the secretary had said. Brognola had discreetly refrained from informing him that if the reports were about the theft of nuclear waste in Louisiana, they probably had most of the information anyway, thanks to the Bear's skill at illegal intercepts.

"Read them," the secretary had said. "Go over them. And when you think you've got the picture, call me and tell me how you propose to handle it."

That surprised Brognola.

Politicians tended to be very cagey, of course, even executives like the secretary of state. They rarely liked to come out and say things like "find the bastards and kill them." Brognola knew that, and he could handle it. But this time the secretary hadn't even said what the situation was that he wanted "handled."

Did he want them to find the missing nuke stuff? Or did he have more specific information on what the hijackers were going to do with it? Usually even the most evasive politicians gave more indication of what they were thinking than the secretary had.

"That depends, Mr. Secretary, on what you want done," Brognola had responded as diplomatically as he could. "How you want whatever it is handled, in other words."

There had been a long silence on the other end of the line. Then, when the secretary spoke again, he was as blunt as he had been evasive earlier. "I want the men stopped. Whatever is necessary to do that. Preferably, kill them. Is that clear enough?"

"That's pretty clear."

"Good."

"One question, though," the Stony Man chief said.

"Yes?"

"What's our timetable? What kind of a deadline are we up against?"

After a pause, the secretary spoke again.
"Listen to this." He read a letter.

To the President
This is an emergency. It's too late for talking.
Only extreme measures will work now. We are the
last of the patriots. America is dying. The nig-
gers and Mexicans and other lower races are
choking her to death. We will stop them. In three
days the Angel of Freedom will eliminate all of
the nonwhite peoples that are taking over our
country. You can't stop us. Nobody can. But
when you see what can be done, you will want to
help us. That is all right if you follow our game
plan. When we are done, America will be great
again.
    Wait for our orders.
                              Aryan Right Coalition


"And get this," the secretary added after he'd read
the text. "The name of the group, Aryan Right Coalition, is signed in flowery handwriting, angling upward, in the center of the text."

"What's that mean?"

"Well, as I see it, the writing looks as if it was designed to imitate John Hancock's signature on the
Declaration of Independence."

"Great," Brognola said with heavy sarcasm. "A
bunch of fascists making a declaration of purification, so to speak, trying to fill the country with only
people like themselves. That ought to be a great place
to live, I *don't* think."

"We think so, too."

"Any idea who?" inquired Brognola.

"The Bureau has put together dossiers on everybody associated with the Aryan Right Coalition. Leader's a guy named Delbert, or Del, Gunther, some giant blond Teutonic fascist from New Orleans."

"New Orleans?"

"Yes. Why?" The secretary's voice came out in a bark. "Does that mean something to you?"

The Stony Man chief hesitated for a second, remembering that he wasn't supposed to know about the hijacking of the nuclear by-products.

Still, he thought, sometimes you have to confess a little to learn a little. Besides, it didn't seem likely the secretary would get too bent out of shape and, if he did, the President would cool him down after a while. It might do him good to wonder how they got hold of the information. Add a little respect and appreciation.

"This wouldn't have any thing to do with a certain hijacking of nuclear waste in Louisiana, would it?"

When the secretary spoke, his voice was deliberately mild. "Now, how in the world did you know about that? Read it in the papers, did you?"

Brognola grinned into the phone. "As my daddy used to say regarding, uh, bedroom activities with the ladies, 'a gentleman *never* tells.'"

"And you're a gentleman?"

"Absolutely."

"I thought you'd say something like that," the secretary responded. "I don't suppose it would do any good to ask you again?"

"I doubt it."

"All right. That's no surprise, either. And, since you asked, yes, it does have something to do with the hijacking of the nuclear material. It has a lot to do with it, in fact. The Aryan Right Coalition or ARC, and Gunther, are the ones that pulled it off.''

The Stony Man chief let out a low whistle. "So that's their play, is it?"

"What?"

"Well, it seems obvious they're going to use the nuclear stuff in their 'purification' exercise. The question is how?"

"How what?"

"How they're going to use the nuclear material. Make a bomb, or what?"

The secretary shook his head, forgetting they were talking on the telephone and Brognola couldn't see him. "No. We've got some experts working on it, though. We'll give you a report when you call again."

"Roger."

"Expect that courier ASAP."

The secretary hung up. The whole conversation had lasted less than five minutes.

Now, the next morning, Able Team was there, all present and accounted for: Lyons, looking, if anything, more tired and bleak than he had when Brognola sent him on the vacation; Blancanales, looking fit but unusually quiet; the irrepressible Gadgets, the only one who seemed to be in his normal, wisecracking frame of mind.

At the far end of the table sat Cowboy Kissinger and Kurtzman. The former was there at Brognola's request; the Bear was present to assist with the briefing.

"How'd they get it?" Lyons inquired.

"Very efficiently. Looks like a well-executed commando operation, probably a small highly trained team." Brognola recounted the facts as he had learned them from the reports prepared by the FBI and the NRC investigators.

It was Kissinger who made the same inquiry Brognola had made the preceding day. "What are they going to do with it, do you figure?"

"Who knows?" Disgust tinged Brognola's voice. "You can't make a bomb out of it, the NRC's panel of experts says. But that's about all they know. All you can do is poison people. Give a whole lot of folks radiation sickness by exposing them to it."

"How would they do that?"

"Nobody on their goddamn blue-ribbon panel of brains seems to know. Oh, they had a few ideas, all right, but nothing that seems very plausible. You can't very well fly over a city and dump the stuff out, but that's about the best they could come up with."

"Beautiful," muttered Kissinger. Brognola shrugged and turned his attention to the next part of the briefing. He was about to begin again when Gadgets spoke up.

"I know how I'd do it," he said pensively.

All heads turned toward him. As the resident genius for the whole Stony Man operation, his opinion carried great weight in matters like this.

In his mid-thirties, Gadgets presented a study in contrasts. He was brilliant, his IQ almost unmeasurable, yet he had never been to college. An expert in the gruesome arts of quiet killing, explosives and guerrilla tactics, he was also a philosopher, able to discuss the theories of war with anybody. Sometimes he wore glasses, other times contact lenses. He looked like a scholar and killed like a soldier.

Electronics and mechanics were his fortes as well as the source of his nickname.

When the computer revolution came along, Gadgets had turned his incredible brain to mastering both the hardware, or actual electronic and mechanical components of computers, and the software, or the programs. He had worked with the Bear to design the Stony Man computer banks. On one occasion, he had reprogrammed Soviet missiles launched at the United States, causing them to detonate harmlessly in the Atlantic Ocean.

So when Gadgets mentioned he might know how the revolutionaries intended to use the nuclear waste, he suddenly had the undivided attention of everybody in the room. He hesitated momentarily, gathering his thoughts.

"So, tell us," urged Kissinger finally. "Or are you waiting for an engraved invitation or something?"

"Water," Gadgets said simply.

A few feet down from him, on the table, was an insulated thermos filled with ice water. Blancanales leaned forward and shoved it down toward Gadgets. "Here," he said.

The Able Team genius grinned and shook his head. "No, I mean water supply. That's how I'd use the radioactive stuff."

"How do you figure?" demanded Kissinger.

"Look at it this way. Say you have a few tons of radioactive waste. Say you're a racist asshole who wants to wipe out a few thousand or a few million nonwhites. How would you do it?"

The question was rhetorical.

Kissinger rolled his eyes. The others knew this was simply one of Gadgets traits. He liked to sort through problems by using the Socratic method, asking a series of questions to frame his thoughts and uncover the truth. It was sometimes maddeningly slow, especially to a "give me the bottom line and let's go kick ass" guy like Kissinger. But the results were usually worth waiting for.

"How would you do it?" Gadgets repeated.

"You tell us," an exasperated Kissinger said.

"First, I'd go someplace where there were lots of the kind of people I want to kill."

"New York," offered the Cowboy with a sigh. He leaned back in his chair and crossed his legs, one ankle on the other knee, reconciling himself to playing the game.

"Good choice. And why is it a good choice?"

"I don't know. Why?"

"Because a city like that has areas with high concentrations of various ethnic groups."

"Ghettos," agreed Kissinger.

"Yes and no. Sometimes they're slums. Other times they're just ethnically concentrated neighborhoods."

"Go on," urged Brognola, intrigued both by Gadgets's reasoning and by the possibility of being able to use his theory to upstage the blue-ribbon panel of experts assembled by the secretary of state.

"What is it that people in those areas need to exist? And sex isn't what I had in mind, guys. Or drugs or rock 'n' roll, either."

"Welfare." The suggestion came from Lyons. His voice was hard and disgusted.

Keeping his face impassive, Brognola regarded the Ironman with concern. Lyons was never exactly a ray of sunshine, but he'd sounded uncharacteristically bitter. The Stony Man chief made a mental note to keep an eye on him. The guy was definitely showing signs of burnout.

Then it struck him. Jesus, he thought. If the guy looks bleak now, wait until I lay the *really* bad news on him. Poor bastard. Nobody's so tough that they can't get the guilts. If a guy was, I'm not sure I'd trust him.

The thought of the news he would soon deliver to his comrade and friend sickened him a little.

If Gadgets saw the same thing in Lyons that Brognola had, he didn't show it. "Not that, either," he said lightly. "I was thinking more of biological necessities, like..."

"Air and water," said Blancanales softly. "*¡Madre de Dios! El agua.* The water."

Gadgets nodded. "It's ideal." He gestured at Brognola. "As *el jefe* said, you can't really dump the stuff out of a plane. You'd get exposed yourself, and it's too indiscriminate. You wouldn't know where the shit would end up."

"But the water..." began the Politician.

"The water is ideal. The water mains are a goddamn grid in the city. What better way to deliver a few radioactive death rays to a specific area than putting it into the water mains that service that area of the city?"

"Jesus," breathed Lyons, coming out of his shell for the first time.

Gadgets nodded. "It would get delivered right to your home. You would drink it, cook with it, bathe in it. It's ideal."

The others thought it over. Then Gadgets added another detail.

"Hell, if you were really sophisticated and had a few guys who worked for the waterworks on your side, you could probably get real specific. Shut off a few mains here, open a few there and pretty much concentrate the stuff in one area. Easily within a few square miles. Maybe within a few blocks, depending on what kind of inside assistance you had. Certainly with enough precision to target areas of—'' he paused, then completed his sentence disgustedly ''—ethnic impurity.''

''Bastards,'' muttered Lyons.

Brognola took that as a good sign. Lyons was starting to focus his anger.

If any single factor drove the Ironman, if there were any particular demon that pursued him, it was his desire for justice. It became almost an obsession at times when he saw the strong maim the weak. And, Brognola knew, Lyons despised the kind of irrational hatred that targeted innocent human beings because of their color or background.

They considered Gadgets's theory in silence. The more they thought about it, the better it sounded. Finally Blancanales spoke.

''What city, amigo?''

Gadgets gave a mild shrug. ''New York, maybe, as Cowboy here suggested. Chicago? Washington, D.C.? Those are the obvious ones. But it doesn't have to be one of them. Hell, if you expand the circle a little, it could be Cleveland, Pittsburgh, Atlantic City. Who knows? But if I had to guess, and it's only a guess, I'd go with New York.''

''Why?''

''Nothing specific. It just feels like some place they'd choose.''

''Why?'' repeated Brognola.

''Maybe because it has historically been a melting pot, a place for the peoples of the world to come. Maybe because the city is to some extent proud of that. Hell, that's what the Statue of Liberty is all about, right?''

The Stony Man chief thought it over. He couldn't say why himself, but somehow he knew that Gadgets was right. New York was it. It had to be.

"The feds have any clue?" Kissinger asked.

"Huh?" The question startled Brognola.

"Does the FBI have any idea where the junk might have been taken? Do they know where we should be looking?"

Brognola allowed a faint smile. "No. But they soon will."

"How so?"

"Because I'll tell 'em." His voice became crisp and businesslike. "In the meantime, I want you guys to be ready to roll. Call it standby if you like. Get your gear together, study the dossiers on the Aryan Right—" he gestured at the papers on the conference room table "—and get some sleep if you can. Any questions?"

There were none.

"All right, let's get on with it." He grimaced. "If we're right, once the feds get a lead on these guys, we're gonna have to be ready to move fast."

"Don't we always?" muttered Lyons. "Hurry up and wait, then do it yesterday."

A grin suddenly spread over Gadgets's face. He spoke louder than normal, pitching his voice in a dramatic imitation of Howard Cosell. "Yes, here they are folks. The Nuclear Assault Team. NAT, for short. A small, hard-hitting, highly mobile assault group, ready to spring into action to recover the missing radioactive isotopes. They're strong. They're tough. They're...." He paused, having run out of adjectives.

Blancanales took up the jest. "Why not RAT?" he asked enthusiastically. "Radioactive Assault Team? Like SWAT."

"Great!" Gadgets rejoined. "Criminals beware—RAT is here. They'll hunt you down. They'll..."

"All right, all right!" Brognola held up his hand, pretending he was annoyed, commanding silence. He got to his feet. "As I said, guys, be ready to roll. I've got a call to make."

**11**

"I need to see you, Carl. Alone."

Lyons paused. Brognola's voice sounded beyond businesslike; it was remote. It struck him as strange for it to be that way, especially in view of their recent banter about possible names and acronyms for the team on this mission.

"Sure, chief. What's on your mind?"

"Not here. Come into my office."

Lyons gave him a searching look, then shrugged. Something was definitely up. Brognola looked so preoccupied that Lyons would be willing to bet whatever was on his mind was not good news.

Brognola led the way into his office and motioned Lyons to close the door.

"So what's up, boss?"

When Brognola turned around, Lyons realized with a start that his chief looked tired and, well, old. For once, the genial, indefatigable, cigar-smoking durability, the booming voice and friendly hand clap on the back weren't there. Instead, he looked as if he had seen and done too much and the cumulative poisons of his work had reached the critical point.

Jesus, thought Lyons, the guy is looking like I feel.

"Everything okay, chief?" he inquired. He felt awkward in that uncertain intimacy that most men feel when trying to express concern about the welfare of another man.

"Oh, I think so, Carl, my boy," he said with a sigh. "It's just been one of those weeks, that's all."

"Yeah, I know what you mean."

Brognola looked at him, then forced a weary smile. "The other guy is definitely ahead on points, if you get my drift. I haven't been knocked out yet, and I don't intend to be, but he's landed a couple of very good shots to the jaw."

Lyons nodded.

Although Brognola was speaking figuratively, the comment reminded Lyons of Maggot and their fist-fight of three days earlier. He gingerly explored the contours of his own jawbone, and winced when he found what he was looking for. It still hurt.

"Yeah," he said again. "I do know what you mean."

No easy way to do it, Brognola decided. He took the straight-ahead approach. "Carl, I think we've located Margaret."

Lyons looked sharply at him. "Where? Is she okay?"

Brognola shook his head. "Mexico. And, if it's her, she's dead."

For an instant, a look of pain crossed Lyons's face like the lash of a whip. Then, just as quickly as it had come, the look vanished. His face became granite-like.

"I'm sorry, Carl," Brognola said gently.

Lyons ignored that. "Any more details?"

"A few. Not many."

"So tell me."

Unconsciously, Brognola moved away, crossing the room, putting distance between himself and Lyons's grief. When Brognola spoke, his voice was tight, formal, deliberately unemotional.

"As soon as we made the possible connection between the stolen nuclear waste and the kidnapping, I put out a BOL on her—a be on the lookout."

"I know what a BOL is, chief."

"Of course. At any rate, I put it out through every federal agency I could think of."

"And?"

"DEA came up with a possible. It came from one of their agents in Mexico. An unidentified white female found by the judicial police near Mexicali. That's in Mexico, near California, I believe. Apparent cause of death, trauma to the head, attributed to a traffic accident. No identification on her. She's in a morgue there now."

"Fingerprints?"

"We can't find any prints to make a comparison."

Lyons looked up, puzzled. Brognola continued.

"She's never been arrested, of course. No passport. Never worked for the government or had a secret clearance of any kind. On her driver's license, she opted not to have a thumbprint."

God bless her, that was Margaret, all right, Lyons thought. She was one of those knee-jerk liberals whose immediate reaction would be that giving a thumbprint on her driver's license was some kind of impermissible invasion of privacy, never mind how it might help straighten out a dozen possible screwups.

Or she had been, anyway, he thought grimly.

"Anything else?"

Brognola shook his head. Lyons turned away and faced the map of the world on the wall. Idly he scanned the continents, until it suddenly occurred to him to try to locate Mexicali. He couldn't find it, however, and supposed it must be too small to be shown on a map of this scale.

"I'll go make the identification," he said at last.

Brognola nodded. "I think it's something you ought to do."

"Yeah, me, too." He sighed. "Hell, I caused it," he said bitterly. "I damn well better be able to go look at it."

"I wasn't thinking that," Brognola replied gently. "There are a number of reasons actually. In fact, I've already had a flight arranged for you. Kurtzman has the details."

"Okay, but what about this other caper? Being on standby?" He tried to force a smile, failed, and abandoned it. "Do you want me to go down there now or wait until something happens here?"

"Now, I think."

"Yeah, I think so, too."

"You can be there and back in a day, or two at the outside. Besides, knowing if it is," Brognola hesitated, then lamely changed his words, "*was* Margaret could be important to the nuclear investigation. Keep your eyes open for anything that might be useful."

"Okay."

"I'm sorry, Carl."

"Yeah."

"I'm also sorry it has to be you that goes down there. If it weren't for how it might affect this mission, I wouldn't be sending you there." He paused, then added, "And I know it might be hard to believe, but it's not your fault."

"Isn't it?"

"No."

Lyons shrugged. "I'll let you know about that when I get back."

"Good luck, Carl."

"Yeah. Sure." Then he softened just a little and added, his voice husky, "I know what you're trying to say, chief. And thanks."

LYONS MOUNTED THE NARROW STEPS and opened the door to the morgue, the *sitio de los muertos*. Behind him, the sidewalk was empty, the three youths vanished.

It was worse than he expected.

A counter ran along the room just inside the door. No more than ten feet separated it from the wall facing the street. Old linoleum in a pattern of yellows, oranges and browns covered the floor. It was cracked and caked with grime. Dirt and thick dust clung stubbornly where the floor met the wall and along the base of the counter. The walls were dirty and dotted with fly specks and brown spots such as might be made by squashing insects.

*¡Madre de Dios!* Lyons thought.

He wondered suddenly why he had chosen that term, the Spanish for "Mother of God."

Blancanales occasionally used it, which was how he knew it. Was it because this was Mexico? When in Rome? Or was it because it somehow fit, not simply blasphemy, but something else, part lament and part supplication?

Whatever, he thought. I've seen bus stations cleaner than this. The thought that Margaret's body might be lying somewhere in a back room in this place sickened him.

The place smelled of must, dirt, stale sweat and something else. An odor permeated the air, as if a beast lurked in the back, crouching, ready to pounce. The odor raised the hairs on the back of his neck in an atavistic way.

It was the smell of death.

A small dark man sat at a desk a few feet beyond the counter, looking at a muscle magazine. Lyons could see the cover photo: a woman in a tiny bathing suit caressed the unreal, bloated muscles of a grinning man, flexing his biceps. Somehow, the magazine seemed like the ultimate insult in this place.

The man hurriedly set down the magazine and approached the counter.

"*¿Sí, señor?*"

"*¿Hablas inglés?* Do you speak English?"

"*No, señor. Pero, espere un momento, por favor.* Please wait."

Without waiting to see what Lyons would do, the little man wheeled and hurried back through a door behind the desk where he had been sitting. He returned a few moments later, towing a thin youth of about fourteen. For a moment, Lyons thought the kid was one of the three loungers from outside, but a closer look showed that he wasn't.

"*Mi hijo.* My son, he speaks," the little man announced proudly.

Lyons looked at the youth. The young man's gaze met his, and in perfect, though stilted and heavily accented English, he inquired, "How may I be of assistance to you, sir?"

"I'm here to see the young woman, American, brown hair. The one with no identification."

The young man looked pained. "Ah, yes. I'm sorry, sir." He spoke with a dignity that seemed genuine and somehow far beyond his years. His pain appeared real.

"Yeah. Well, anyway, I'd like to take a look at her."

"Of course. I will show you myself."

The youth moved to the gate by the counter, and Lyons walked toward it, prepared to enter and be escorted into the back. To his surprise, the kid came through the gate himself, almost running into the Ironman in the process.

He gestured to the front door. "It is outside, sir."

Lyons shrugged and followed him out the door and onto the sidewalk. They turned right and walked along the front of the building, then turned right again in the alley where the structure ended.

A narrow flight of rickety wooden stairs led up the wall of the building to the second floor.

Jesus, thought Lyons, what a dump. I'm sorry, Margaret.

The young man opened the door and beckoned Lyons to enter. He stepped inside, then waited as his escort shut the door and walked around ahead of him.

"Wait here, please."

The youth disappeared into the back. Lyons heard the protesting squeak of unoiled metal on metal. It was followed by a heavy thump. He didn't dare speculate about the sound. There were more noises, then silence.

A few moments later the young man emerged.

He was pushing a makeshift gurney. It looked as if somebody had taken a shopping cart from a supermarket and mounted a piece of plywood a couple of feet wide and six feet long on top of it. On closer inspection, he saw that was exactly what it was. Holes had been drilled in the wood to accommodate the wires that secured it to the cart.

A dirty sheet covered the obviously human form on the plywood slab. The sheet was too short, and the feet stuck out at one end, pathetically small and vulnerable.

Margaret had had small feet. It had been a joke between them. Lyons knew right then what he would see when the sheet was removed.

He moved to the side of the gurney.

The youth reached up and took hold of the sheet. Then, with a concern and professionalism that belied the meanness of the surroundings, he gently turned it down.

Lyons caught his breath. For an instant, the room swirled and he thought crazily that he might faint.

He didn't, of course. He had seen too much death for that—too much of which he had engineered himself. He had been there and back, and he'd thought he'd seen it all. In fact, until that instant he would have said his ability to grieve, to be moved by death, had itself died, a casualty of his profession.

Still, nothing could have prepared him for this.

Her face was gone.

Where her face had been was covered with a handkerchief. It looked clean and sparkling white, he thought. But beneath the thin cloth was the darkness of ruined flesh rather than the lighter pale of skin.

"She was terribly injured in the accident, *señor*. I'm afraid there is not much of her face to see."

Lyons steeled himself. His mind on autopilot, his emotions locked away, he reached forward and removed the handkerchief.

The kid was right. No help there.

With a pathologist's detachment, he thought of other ways to make the identification. *Any identifying marks or scars, Mr. Lyons?* Why, yes, there's a burn scar on her lower leg, her ankle actually, where she touched it up against the hot muffler of my motorcycle about a million years ago. *Anything else you can think of?* Yeah, a little white crater of a scar about an eighth of an inch across under one arm, towards the back, where she had a mole removed. *Let's take a look, shall we?*

Lyons moved to the other end of the gurney to check the ankle, but he already knew what he would find.

He found it.

With a sigh, he started to check for the scar under the arm but realized he would have to turn the stiffened form over on the narrow board and bend the chilled arm away from the side to do it. It wasn't that he didn't have the stomach for the task; rather, it just wasn't necessary after he'd seen the irregular patch of scar tissue on the ankle.

Goodbye, Margaret. I'm sorry. Goodbye.

His movements wooden, Lyons replaced the sheet.

He asked the kid a few questions, gaining what sparse details he could on how and where she had been found, where he could get a copy of any official reports. He asked to see the clothing she had been wearing when her body was found, and he examined it. Then he gave the kid a thousand dollars U.S. to have the body shipped to a mortuary in Los Angeles and kept there for two weeks. Normally he wouldn't have trusted that his directions would be carried out, but at gut level he had faith in the youth.

Then he realized there wasn't anything left to do. The drill was over.

The young man called for a taxi to take Lyons to the San Ysidro border crossing, where he could get another cab to the San Diego airport.

Lyons felt somehow flattened, numbed by an emotional overload. He responded to it by attempting to trivialize the day's events, as though they were dry facts devoid of feeling.

What the hell, he thought. All in a day's work. It goes with the territory. You gonna juggle plates, you gonnna break a few, Ironman. That's the way it is.

Sure. Right on. Kinda tough on the ones you break, though.

You can't take it, go sell insurance or something. You want to run with the big dogs, you better be ready to piss up tall trees. We need guys who do what you do. Otherwise, the germs will take over. Besides, it's what you do best. Even if you do break a few plates.

Yeah, I know. I'm just sorry I broke this one.

Goodbye, Margaret.

## 12

When Lyons got back to Stony Man Farm, the rest of the team was gone.

"Where are they? Something break on the nuclear caper?"

Brognola nodded. "Later. First give me your report."

Lyons did. When he had finished, the Stony Man chief grimaced. "Not much, is it?"

"No. But it's all there is."

Brognola thought that over. "I suppose so. For now, anyway. I'd hoped for something that might tell us why, or how she happened to end up in Mexico."

Lyons shook his head. "Nothing, boss. Not that I can tell, anyway. If it's there, I didn't see it."

The Stony Man chief shrugged. "We'll tie it all together somehow. Sooner or later."

"Yeah."

Lyons wondered if Brognola was just saying that for his benefit as a sort of gesture of sympathy, or if he really intended to follow through with an investigation if it turned out that Margaret's death was not related to their main mission.

The former would be more logical, he realized.

Strictly speaking, the personal vendettas of team members weren't what the Stony Man concept was all about. This was so, he realized, even though it was a quest for personal vengeance—against the Mafia extortionists responsible for his family's death—that had launched Mack Bolan into this business in the first place.

Then he decided it didn't really matter. If it was merely a gesture, it was a good one.

Besides, whether Brognola meant it or not, Lyons did.

Yes, Margaret, wherever you are, we *will* tie it up. We'll figure it out, add up the columns of figures, balance the books a little. We'll get to the bottom line. And when we do, I'll settle the account.

"Carl."

It's like a rope stretching off into the distance, Margaret. It goes through swamps and jungles and disappears way up ahead into the mists. Maybe it goes down into hell itself. But I *will* follow it out, hand over hand if need be, until I come to the end.

"Lyons!"

And I will get to the end. I swear to God I will. And when I find out who's there, I'll see to it that he wears that rope. Around his neck. And I'll pull him off the ground with it, up into the air, kicking and jerking. And I'll watch him die.

It'll be a pleasure.

It won't bring you back. I know that. It might not even ease my guilt. And you probably wouldn't even have wanted me to do it. But I'm gonna do it, anyway. Because it's something that has to be done.

"Ironman, snap out of it, for God's sake."

With a start, Lyons realized that Brognola had been talking to him, saying his name. He hadn't heard it, not consciously, anyway, he had been so lost in his thoughts of vengeance. *There's a message there* he thought suddenly. *Don't let your thirst for revenge prevent you from seeing what's going on around you, Ironman. Or you might not live to find the end of that rope.*

"Sorry, boss. I was thinking about something, I guess."

"No shit, Lyons. You were a million miles away."

"Sorry, I said. What's going on with the nuclear caper?"

Eyes narrowed, Brognola looked at him, trying to determine just how close to the ragged edge his best man was. "FBI located them. I sent Blancanales and Schwarz there. Oh, yes, and Kissinger, too, pending your return."

"Where are they?"

Brognola gave a thin smile. "New York, of all places. How about that?"

"How about that, indeed?" echoed Lyons.

"Yeah. Our boy Gadgets was right on the money, as usual. You know that blue-ribbon commission of brains the secretary of state assembled to study this and figure out how and where these dipshits might be going to use this stuff? Well, I stuck it right up their high-IQ asses on this one."

"So tell me. Where are they? What's going on? Let's get going, chief."

"Need a fight, do you, Lyons? Never mind." He grinned at his ace warrior. It was not a very pleasant grin. "Here's the story."

As Brognola explained it, the secretary's panel hadn't thought too highly of Gadgets's theory. Too conjectural, they'd said. Sheer speculation, they'd called it.

"Never mind the fact that they didn't have any better ideas, conjectural or otherwise," snorted Brognola. "The secretary's a good man, of course, don't get me wrong there, but his little panel— Sometimes these Ivy League tight asses make me want to puke.

"At any rate, it seemed the FBI thought Gadgets's theory was pretty good. So they began nosing around New York and, incidentally, started checking out all trucks headed that way from Louisiana."

"How'd they do that?" Lyons asked.

"They began by checking all the records for tractor trailers—at every state line, inspection station, weighing station and official checkpoint on all the major routes to New York. Then they worked backward, confirming that each rig was legit. That meant contacting every company shown on the records as having a rig in the area and asking them to confirm it."

Lyons let out a low whistle. "Pretty impressive. Lotta manpower in that."

Brognola nodded. "Damn right. Remember, though, that this is the FBI working with God knows how many other agencies, both local and federal. And when they pull out the stops, and if everybody from the Supreme Court to the American Civil Liberties Union isn't trying to tell them how to do their job—"

"Don't forget sister Sue's sewing circle," Lyons interrupted.

As a cop in Los Angeles, before his affiliation with Stony Man, he had experienced the restraints Brognola was referring to. He knew too well the waste and nonsense that inevitably resulted when groups such as those Brognola had mentioned tried to run the executive branch.

"Right. Either they aren't meddling, or the Bureau is for once ignoring them," agreed Brognola. "At any rate, without all that crap to tie them down, they are the best in the world. By far."

"And that's what's going on here?"

"This borders on national emergency time, remember. What would you do if you were the director of the FBI and the secretary of state told you to produce or else?"

"Good point."

"At any rate," Brognola continued, "they hit pay dirt. An Atlantic Richfield Company tank truck went through every checkpoint on the main route from Louisiana north to New York. The timing was right, too. Only it wasn't an ARCO truck at all, it turns out. ARCO didn't have a truck like that on the road. A company like that keeps pretty good track of all its rigs, and they were all present and accounted for, where they ought to be."

"Except this one," guessed Lyons.

"You got it. But that's not the half of it."

Excitement surged through the Ironman. "What is it, then? Tell me, for God's sake."

A look of grim satisfaction crossed Brognola's face. "I told you we'd tie it together with Margie's death and all. Well, we haven't got there yet, but we're close."

"So tell me, goddamn it!"

"The rig, the phony ARCO truck, had two men driving it. We think it was the two you rousted in San Francisco. The two bikers. Maggot and Mikey."

Lyons stared. "No shit?" he demanded incredulously. "Are you sure, boss?"

"Ninety percent sure." Then Brognola waved his hand irritably, though his irritation was directed at himself. "What am I saying? Hell, we're sure. The descriptions match. And an FBI handwriting guy analyzed some of the chicken scratchs on the sign-in logs at a couple of inspection points. Compared them to handwriting samples from their prison records. Said he could tell, quote, to a reasonable certainty, unquote, that it was the same guy."

"Jesus," Lyons breathed. "So there *is* a connection."

"Between the nuclear hijacking and Margie? Looks like it."

"When do I leave, boss?"

"You need to know where you're going first."

"Right. Where am I going?"

"New York. Upstate. An abandoned sawmill outside Troy. That's about three hours north of New York City."

"What are they doing there?"

Brognola shrugged. "We don't know, for sure. The speculation is that they're staging up there, getting ready to do whatever they're going to do with the isotopes."

"Has that been determined for sure yet? Does it look like what Gadgets thought? The water supply?"

"We don't know." The Stony Man chief let out a sigh and stared at the floor for a few moments. "On one hand, I have to go with Gadgets's theory. After all, he was dead on target with the location. On a gut level, that gives some credibility to the rest of his theory."

"But?"

"But on the other hand, who the hell knows what these goddamn crazies are going to do with it? Other than that it's going to be directed at 'purifying' the white race." Brognola's voice was bitter. "Well, one thing's for sure, assholes like this are living proof that the race needs purifying, though I don't think that's what they had in mind."

Lyons didn't respond.

After a moment, Brognola looked up at him. "There'll be a chopper here in twenty minutes. Be ready. It'll take you up there so you can hook up with the other guys."

"Ten four, chief." Then a thought occurred to Lyons. He didn't even know what their orders were. He asked Brognola.

A smile tugged at the corners of Brognola's mouth. "Do you want me to tell you what the secretary of state told me when I asked him the same question?"

Lyons shrugged. "Sure."

"He wanted us to, quote, handle it, unquote."

"That's it?"

"No. I pinned the political bastard down then, and, to his credit, he came through."

"What did he do?"

"Got off the fence, said he wanted them stopped." Brognola tipped his head back and rolled his eyes upward. "'Whatever is necessary to do that. Preferably kill them. Is that clear enough?' Yes that's what he said."

Lyons said nothing.

Brognola looked at him with a smile. "Well, Ironman. Is that clear enough for you, too?"

"That's pretty clear."

A grin split Brognola's face and suddenly he was again the durable, cigar-smoking leader that Lyons knew him to be, a cheerful Winston Churchill, always there, always strong, always in control. "Funny thing, Ironman. Those were my exact words to him. Any questions?"

"No, sir."

"Good. Those are your orders."

Lyons got up to leave. Brognola called him back.

"One more thing, Ironman."

"Yes, chief?"

"The Stony Man operation does not exist for the purpose of vindicating our own individual injustices. In other words, we aren't in business to make you feel all better by giving you a hair shirt and letting you rub ashes in your hair and kill everybody in sight who might have been involved in something you feel responsible for. We don't go in for shit like that. And if you're ever given a subpoena to testify before some goddamn congressional committee about our activities, you can say that. Right?"

"Absolutely right, chief."

"On the other hand, I've always thought that morale is important in any outfit. Don't you agree?"

Lyons grinned, then adopted a deadpan expression. He knew what was coming.

This was a ritual he and Brognola had been through before, though it was never exactly the same any two times in a row. It also served the useful purpose of reminding him that the mission was indeed more important than the man, although there could be a certain latitude in applying that principle.

"Yes, chief. Morale is important, all right. Extremely important."

"I thought you'd say that, somehow." When Lyons didn't respond, he continued. "With that in mind, I'll remind you that our primary mission is stopping these white-power crazies and whatever their plans are with respect to the hot nuke stuff."

"Yes, sir."

"However, if in the course of so doing, you are in a position to, shall we say, settle some other delinquent accounts, then settling those accounts would probably be beneficial to morale."

"Extremely beneficial."

"And now it appears that Margie's death is related somehow to the folks involved in the nuclear hijack. That being the case—" Brognola was even more deadpan than Lyons "—why, I'd consider settling those accounts to be within the scope of your mission, wouldn't you?"

"Yes, sir. Completely within the scope, I'd say."

"Impossible to separate. Part and parcel of the same thing, the way I see it."

"Yes, sir. Exactly the same."

"Good. You have your orders, then."

Lyons turned to go.

"Oh, one more thing, Carl." Brognola was taking out a cigar as he spoke. He licked it, bit off the tip with his canine teeth and lit it.

"Yes, sir?"

"You're not in the police department anymore."

"No, sir."

"In settling those accounts, remember the drawbacks inherent in our criminal justice system, God bless it. You of all people should know those shortcomings." Brognola blew a cloud of gray smoke as he spoke.

"Yes, sir."

"Trials cost a lot of taxpayers' money. They're time-consuming and require witnesses. And if there was a trial then, next you know, some tight-ass shyster defense lawyer will start cross-examining you about Stony Man Farm and Mack Bolan and a bunch of stuff it's not their business to know about."

"Not their business," agreed Lyons.

"And courts of law sometimes turn criminals free for the damnedest reasons." He paused and puffed on his cigar. "When I say settle the accounts, I'm not talking about arresting the perpetrators. You get my drift?"

"Ten four, sir."

"Good. Now get going."

A sudden grin split Lyons's deadpan expression. "RAT One, over and out."

## 13

"Here's the plan."

With Lyons engaged in his own grim mission down in Mexico, Brognola had designated Blancanales in charge until the Ironman's return.

It was a good choice. Though any of the men could have done it, the Politician had fought with Mack Bolan in Vietnam, and, next to Lyons, was the most seasoned commando on the team.

As squad leader, Blancanales should have stood by and called the shots, not played them. But he was the best at jungle recon, so he made the initial survey of the sawmill where the hijackers were supposedly holed up.

It had been just after noon when the chopper had deposited the three men in the heavily forested area some twenty miles outside Troy, in upstate New York. They had put down approximately five miles from the sawmill and had trekked in on foot. "Humping," as Blancanales and Gadgets called it, using the term that had been popular among ground troops in Vietnam.

Any observer who had happened to see them would have thought that the scene itself could have come from Nam.

The three men wore camouflage fatigues and flak jackets. Each carried an M-16, the mainstay U.S. infantry weapon, a .223 caliber, ass-kicking carbine capable of semi or fully automatic fire. "Auto-burn," as Blancanales called it. Each man also carried a Colt Government Model .45 pistol, as modified and improved by Kissinger. Nothing major, just some smoothing here, some honing there and a different spring or two.

A good, rugged weapon became a hell of a fine one.

In addition, Blancanales and Gadgets carried pouches of grenades, including antipersonnel and flash-bangs, and several low- and medium-opening flares. All of them carried several extra clips for both the M-16s and the .45s.

Camouflage paint for their faces and hands completed the preparations.

They had staged up about a thousand yards from the old mill. It had been midafternoon when Blancanales, the jungle warfare expert, had headed into the bush—Indian country—to do his recon. When he'd returned, it was pushing dusk.

Now he spread a topographic map out before them as he spoke. The map covered an area of several square miles. Blancanales swiftly inked in four rectangles below a river that ran diagonally across the map from upper right to lower left.

The former Green Beret pointed to the largest rectangle, which also happened to be the uppermost one as they looked at the map.

"This large one is the sawmill itself," he said. "Or what used to be, anyway. There's only machinery left now. It's north of this warehouse." He indicated the location of the building on the map as he spoke. "From our perspective, it's behind the warehouse."

"This place is abandoned, right?" inquired the Cowboy. "It's not in use as a paper mill or whatever anymore?"

Blancanales nodded. "As I said, the equipment north of the warehouse—it's actually like a big old barn, made out of splintery boards—is mainly dismantled. Brognola said it was a sawmill, but that's strictly a guess. It just looks like that. At any rate, it's all overgrown and abandoned."

"How fucking rustic," muttered Kissinger in a cynical voice.

"Quaint," agreed Gadgets with a wink. "Pastoral. Bucolic, even."

Blancanales looked at his two companions as though they had lost their minds. "Yeah," he finally said. "And in the middle of it sits God knows how many tons of nuclear waste."

"You saw the truck, then?" asked Kissinger excitedly.

"I think so."

The Cowboy wrinkled his brow. "What the hell do you mean, you think so? Either you did or you didn't, right? I mean, it's not like it looks rustic or anything. It's a big fucking tractor trailor with a big shiny tank and it probably says ARCO on it. Did you see it or didn't you?"

Gadgets rolled his eyes and wondered if the Politician was going to try to find out if Kissinger's head screwed on or snapped on. By removing it.

Blancanales regarded the Cowboy with something decidedly less than affection. The former narcotics agent had a nonstop, abrasive good humor. That was all well and good, but at times it could get on the nerves.

This was one of those times.

Besides, something else was troubling the Politician about Kissinger. Though he had no doubt that the Cowboy was tough and courageous, the fact remained that he was still an unknown quantity in many respects.

He ran over the facts in his mind.

Sure, Kissinger knew weapons. Hell, he ought to. He had worked free-lance and as a consultant for some of the biggest names in the business: Colt, Beretta, Heckler & Koch, IMI. He was an expert in weapons design, especially handguns. What he didn't know about pistols of all sorts would probably fit on a postcard. And he knew how to use them; Blancanales had seen that on the ranges, in the shoot–don't shoot exercises and the simulation drills they had been through together.

Okay so the guy could shoot.

But, Blancanales also knew that Kissinger didn't have the combat background that he and Gadgets possessed, even though Kissinger, too, had been in Nam. Most of his experience had been in law enforcement, though not as a city policeman as Lyons had been.

The Cowboy had been an agent with the old Bureau of Narcotics and Dangerous Drugs, one of the forerunners of the Federal Drug Enforcement Administration. It had been an outfit widely known for its freewheeling, high, wide and handsome tactics.

"Crash doors, kick ass and take names" had in many cases seemed to be the only approved procedure of the BNDD.

"Constitutional rights? What constitutional rights?" had been their working slogan.

Not that Kissinger hadn't been in his share of tight spots in his time. Blancanales recognized that it took a set of *jhuevos* to do the stuff that had been the BNDD's stock in trade. Though he had never been a cop himself, the Politician recalled a couple of instances in which Able Team had been called upon to use the legal approach before resorting to what Brognola termed the "extralegal" methods that were *their* stock in trade.

The Politician hadn't liked it. Not one little bit.

He remembered having to do it by the book on a search warrant. Talk about being a target, a sitting duck in a shooting gallery. Doing it by the book meant walking up to the door of a house that might contain killers who had nothing to lose, knocking on the door and announcing who you were and why you were there and then breaking in.

Not fun, he thought. Hell, even when a man wasn't operating under those kinds of legal restrictions, building entries were a real sphincter-tightener. Anybody who had ever done house-to-house urban guerrilla warfare knew the feeling.

Just ask the marines who'd been in Beirut, or any of the GIs in Vietnam. Or, for that matter the cops in Watts or Detroit.

And Kissinger had done that sort of stuff a lot with the BNDD, so he was no pussy. It was where he got his nickname, Cowboy, in fact. Still, the very rough-riding characteristics that had made him something of a minor legend in BNDD circles also made his personality somewhat abrasive at times. But none of that altered the fact that he didn't have combat experience, and that troubled Blancanales.

Of course, the same could have been said about Lyons when he joined the Stony Man operation. On paper, the Ironman had possessed even less of what it took than Kissinger. He'd had no military experience, no boot camp, no airborne, no hours on the clock of slogging it out in the jungles and rice paddies. Just a dozen years in law enforcement, from street cop to a member of an elite organized crime strike force. And a set of nuts made of stainless steel.

In the final analysis, maybe that was what it took.

Blancanales determined he'd given Kissinger the benefit of the doubt. He'd watch Kissinger in combat, see how he did, and for now assume he could do it.

And, having so decided, he wouldn't let Kissinger's mannerisms get under his skin.

Looking at Cowboy, Blancanales realized he was right. It was just part of the guy's rough-shod personality. Still, a little reinforcement of the pecking order might not be entirely inappropriate.

Quick as a flash, he leaned forward and popped the Cowboy on the cheek with his fingertips. It wasn't hard, to be sure, but it wasn't exactly soft, either. And he did it with blurring speed, faster than a snake's strike.

Kissinger, though quick himself, came up with nothing but empty air when he grabbed for the Politician's hand, which by then was back by the Politician's side.

"Sorry, amigo. Looked like a fly on your cheek. I missed him, though."

Blancanales spoke with mock seriousness, then gave a broad, easy, Politician grin. Before Kissinger could get angry, Blancanales quickly continued, "And, *sí*, amigo, I do know what the truck looks like. What I mean is this. I saw the tractor inside this big shed. I think. I couldn't get close enough to see the whole thing or even get a good look at it, but I'm reasonably sure that at least the tractor part is there."

Gadgets calmly watched the two men.

Kissinger's eyes had narrowed dangerously as he'd instinctively touched his stinging cheek. Blancanales was still grinning his broad, easy grin. However, his brown eyes were watchful and hard. Yes, indeed, this could be interesting, Gadgets thought. Could be a hell of a fight.

At six two and two hundred, Kissinger had a size advantage over the stocky ex-Green Beret: he was significantly taller and some fifteen pounds heavier. He was also quick and strong. But Gadgets knew that Blancanales was incredibly strong. Moreover he was heavier than Kissinger in proportion to height and had better leverage. Besides, the former Green Beret was trained and proficient to an awe-inspiring degree in the fighting arts.

All in all, Gadgets gave the edge to the Politician. Still, it could be interesting.

This wasn't the time for it, though. Blancanales would know that, but Kissinger might not.

"All right, all right, you guys," he interjected genially. "You're tougher than shit. Hell on two legs, both of you. But let's save it for these assholes here," he said, gesturing in the direction of the sawmill. "Then if there's any left over, you can try it out on each other."

For a moment, there was no change. Then Kissinger relaxed and grinned. "Next time you see a fly, make sure you at least get the SOB. It's the least you could do. Hell, I'd do the same for you."

It wasn't exactly a peace treaty, Gadgets thought. The closing comment, about doing the same for you, signified possible resumption of the festivities at some future time. Still, it was at least a truce, a cease-fire. Besides, knowing his personality, Gadgets guessed the Cowboy would let it pass, forgetting about it by the time all this was over.

The tension gone, Gadgets added a sarcastic afterthought before turning back to the map. "Fucking Brognola," he muttered. "Gives me two trained attack dogs, puts them in the same cage and expects they aren't gonna bite each other."

"As I was saying, amigos," Blancanales continued, "there are three other buildings to be aware of. Down here, at seven o'clock—assuming we put the sawmill building at twelve—is an old house. Wood, two story, boarded up. And over here, call it four and five o'clock, are two smaller outbuildings. Both wood, both falling apart."

"Where are the dirt bags?" inquired Kissinger, the earlier incident apparently forgotten.

"Looks like they've taken over the old house." Blancanales pointed at the rectangle at seven o'clock.

"How many?"

The Politician shook his head. "Hard to say. I counted seven, but I'd have to guess there are more inside."

"Why?"

"I could hear noises from inside, like somebody was there. I'd say there's a small but undetermined number more than the seven I saw. Maybe two or three more.''

Not good odds, thought Gadgets. Especially when they had the high ground. Aloud, he said, ''So what's the plan?''

Blancanales shrugged. ''Move in and take over. That truck of hot stuff is number one priority. We get it, the crisis is over. The rest is only mopping up.''

They considered that. Finally Kissinger spoke. ''Sounds great to me. Hell, kick ass and take names. Shoot everything that moves and arrest 'em later. One thing, though.''

''What's that?''

''Why not get some reinforcements? Hell, call in an air strike, shoot the shit out of 'em, then move in.''

Blancanales nodded. ''Good point. But it would be impossible to keep that sort of thing low key. And that's the whole reason it's us instead of the AirCav.''

''What do you mean?''

''Secrecy, man,'' explained Gadgets. ''Soldiers sometimes talk, even the best of them. We don't. All things being equal, by that I mean assuming we can do it, the guys at the top would prefer to have us, for security reasons. Besides,'' he said, grinning, ''if they ever worried about *us* talking, there's fewer of us to kill.''

Kissinger stared at him. ''Great. Far fucking out. For a moment there, I almost thought you meant that.''

''Maybe I did.''

Blancanales interrupted at this point. ''Here's the plan. We'll approach from the southeast, from behind the two old sheds at four and five o'clock. We'll check the place out, get a feel for who's where.''

"They'll probably be in the main house, won't they?" suggested Kissinger.

"Probably. But some of them could be in the big barn. Either staying there or standing watch. I doubt anybody will be in the two old sheds, though, which is why I've chosen that approach."

"When do we do it? Wait until dark?" asked the Cowboy.

Blancanales shook his head. "Negative. I figure right now."

"Why so? Won't night be better cover for us?"

"Yes. But also for them. I figure now is ideal. The best we'll get, anyway. It's gloomy enough to afford some cover, better than daylight, anyway. But we'll still have some light to operate by. Besides, at night they'll probably post some kind of guard. But they'll probably wait until darkness to do it. So if we do it now, we avoid that."

Kissinger thought it over. "Sounds good to me."

Blancanales looked at his two companions. "Let's hump."

## 14

They couldn't have timed it better.

Blancanales in the lead, Kissinger second and Gadgets bringing up the rear, they moved silently up to the southernmost of the two tumbledown outbuildings.

The former jungle warfare expert glanced around him. *Bueno,* he thought. The lighting was in that stage of uneasy twilight where a man could see adequately if he looked hard but not if he just glanced around. It was great if a man had the advantage of surprise and lousy if he didn't.

Turning to Kissinger and Gadgets, Blancanales mouthed, "Wait here." Then, keeping low, he moved silently to their right, toward the corner of the building, so he could survey the house and the warehouse.

Just as he neared the corner, a tall, lean man carrying a compact machine gun—an Uzi or a MAC-10 by the look of it—came around from the other direction.

The two men ran squarely into each other.

"What the hell...!" The startled exclamation burst from the tall man's throat.

"Shit!" Blancanales spat the oath in a disgusted hiss. Then without hesitation, he sprang forward as though propelled by a powerful spring.

He clapped one hand, his left one, over the man's mouth. With a desperation born of survival instinct, he dug his thumb and fingers into either cheek in a vicelike grip. Then, using his right hand—formed into a martial arts striking configuration, fingers stiff, reinforced by the thumb—he drove a paralyzing blow into the man's solar plexus. It hit just below the sternum. Blancanales's rigid fingers concentrated the impact an inch or two below the man's flexible cartilage where the ribs joined, transmitting the shock into his diaphragm and the organs below.

"Aarghh!" A paralyzed grunt, half cry and half groan, exploded from the man's twisted mouth between Blancanales's fingers. The tall man's muscles went rigid from the force of the blow, and he went over backward with Blancanales on top of him.

The Politician scrambled forward to maintain his position and his grip on the man's mouth. With his right hand, he snatched a combination dagger and survival knife from his belt and drove it into the small of the man's back.

Nerve circuits overloaded and died. The man gave a final spasm, arching his body as though trying to bend backward around the blade.

Maybe it was just reflex, caused by the dying surge to the nervous system. Maybe it was the brain, dead but not willing to admit it, that sent a last message down the man's arm to his fist.

Then again, maybe it was sheer bad luck.

A single shot rang out from the compact machine gun clenched in the man's right hand. It cut through the evening forest sounds and died away like a sonic boom.

"Fuck!"

The oath burst from Kissinger. He and Gadgets sprinted toward the Politician, who was scrambling to his feet, bloody dagger clenched in his right fist.

In the gloom, neither Gadgets nor the Cowboy saw the blood that drenched their comrade's right leg, a few inches above the knee.

"Quick!" Blancanales snapped. "Cowboy, you take the warehouse. We'll take the house. Gadgets, you go left. I'll go right." Then, as one, the three men dashed around the corner and sprinted between the two abandoned sheds toward their respective destinations.

Even as they did so, shouts and the sounds of activity reached them from the house.

Drawing on the patterns he'd run as a wide receiver, Kissinger angled for the large shed at the back of the property.

Orange flames burst from the porch of the house, accompanied by the persistent hammering of a machine gun. It sounded like a 9 mm, probably another Uzi or MAC-10, modified to fire full-auto.

Puffs of dirt exploded from the impact as the gun stitched a line behind the running Cowboy. As fast as Kissinger was, the line of bullets was faster as the gunman swiveled his aim to track the sprinting figure.

"Eeee-ya-hoo!"

The high-pitched yell of exhilaration tore from the Cowboy's throat as he ran. At the last instant, just as the line of bullets was closing the gap, Kissinger made a sharp cut to his right and dove for the cover of an old log.

The row of slugs went on by, slicing through where he should have been but wasn't.

By the time the gunman realized he'd missed, Kissinger was nowhere to be seen.

In the meantime, Blancanales had got a fix on the gunman. He slowed his limping run and threw his M-16 to his shoulder. The sharp, short burst was dead on target.

"Yeah!" Blancanales exclaimed in a guttural grunt of satisfaction as he fired. It was one of those bursts that a man can call; it simply *felt* like it was just right.

And it was. Center punch. Ten ring. A .223 KO.

The gunman flipped over backward from the impact of the slugs in the meat and ribs of his chest. His weapon clattered to the floor.

A heavy crash followed by the sound of wood splintering came from the house. The sound seem to come from high up. As he increased his speed again, still limping heavily, Blancanales cast a quick glance upward.

A sheet of plywood that had been used to board up one of the upstairs windows was bowed outward. Another crash came from inside, then another, and the plywood suddenly came free and dropped to the ground. The shadowy figure of a man appeared at the window. He was holding something dark.

Somehow, Blancanales didn't for an instant think it was an umbrella.

For the man in the window the angle was perfect. For Blancanales, though, it was no-win.

He could see all the possibilities as if in a slow motion film.

If he could make it to the house, he could flatten himself against the wall. Then he would be able to move right or left until the guy leaned out to try to shoot downward. And when he did, he would be a sitting duck.

There was only one thing wrong. The Politician knew he would never make it to the house before the man above him cut loose with the 9 mm, or whatever weapon he happened to have.

Instantly he reviewed his choices.

When the chances are slim and none, a man goes with slim. Slim meant trying to beat the other man to the punch, halting his forward momentum—which meant making himself a perfect target—and trying to bring up his M-16 to get off the first burst.

The Politician could feel the man's sights settling on him. He could visualize exactly what the man would be seeing: the crude metal sights of the machine gun steadying on the camouflage-garbed man below who was trying to raise his own gun. The terrorist would know he had the advantage, that there was no hurry as long as he didn't get careless. Then the trigger finger would clamp down, and a hail of 9 mm death would angle downward. . . .

Slim wasn't going to get it. The Politician knew that. The other guy would get a burst off before the Politician could level his M-16 at the target.

Fuck it!

Just fuck it! It's never over until it's over. Who said that? No matter. It isn't over yet. When the shattered body can no longer pull the trigger, when the brain can no longer give the message and when the spirit gives up—*then* it's over. But not until then. Never until then.

For now, go for the slim chance.

He heard the burst of autoburn. And he knew it hadn't come from his own weapon, which he was still raising to try to get it on target. Part of his mind stiffened his body against the impending shock of the impact, willing himself to stay on his feet and to keep trying to get on target, even if he got hit and hit hard.

Better to die trying than to just die.

In the dim light, he saw the man's head come apart.

It was too dark to see it all in living color, but he did see the man's head snap backward and the patch of light color that was his face suddenly turn dark. And somehow he either saw or imagined he saw the exploding dark colors behind the man as skull and blood and brain blasted outward.

"Eeee-ya-hoo!"

The exhilarated war whoop came from somewhere behind the Politician, and he knew without looking that the Cowboy had saved his bacon, that the burst of autofire had come from the Cowboy rather than from the man above.

That deserved some recognition, the Politician thought. Hell, he'd just gotten a freebie; by rights, he ought to have been dead right now. And, since he wasn't, he decided he might as well push his luck a little, ride it hard, then put it away wet.

It was in every logical sense a stupid thing to do. He knew that. But in the crazy unreality of combat, it made sense. It was like unexpectedly winning a jackpot. A jackpot is all found money in a sense, so a man might as well throw a little away.

Take a gamble.

He stopped in his tracks and turned toward the Cowboy.

Then heedless of the fact that he was making himself a perfect target, the Politician gave a formal bow in that direction and followed it with a jaunty salute.

"Eeeee-ya-hooo!" came Kissinger's war whoop again, acknowledging the Politician's gestures.

Then, and only then, did the Politician turn and race once again toward the house.

The window gave him an idea. As he ran, his fingers scrabbled in his pouch for a grenade. He found one, activated it and lobbed it in a high, easy arc into the upstairs window where moments before his would-be killer had been.

He didn't wait for results. Immediately after the grenade left his fingers, Blancanales looked quickly to his right, toward the rear of the house.

Nothing.

Then, as the seconds ticked off on his mental clock, he moved quickly to his left, toward the front of the house, where Gadgets had gone.

A long, low wooden porch ran along the entire front of the house. At one time a railing had bordered the wooden floor. Now only the splintered remains of uprights and a single horizontal board remained.

As the Politician peeked around the corner, he saw Gadgets break from the cover of a derelict car that sat some twenty feet in front of the porch. Gadgets was firing as he ran, charging the porch at a dead run.

Gadgets made a running leap for the porch. Then, in the first of a bewildering jumble of events, Blancanales saw a movement on the far end of the porch, to Gadgets's extreme left. The Politician started to swing his M-16 in that direction, then realized his partner was in the way.

There was nothing Blancanales could do but watch helplessly as Gadgets fell heavily to the ground in front of the porch just as the man at the far end opened up with an automatic weapon.

A split second later, the muffled boom of the grenade going off in the upstairs room where the Politician had tossed it shook the house.

## 15

When the dying enemy's gun went off and Blancanales hissed his commands to take the house, Gadgets had streaked for the front of the ramshackle structure, some forty yards ahead. Then he had seen the rusting car body and had recognized it for what it was.

Cover.

Rather than angling straight for the house, he altered his course to the left so that he could run up behind the car. He was assisted in making this decision by the sudden appearance of a shadowy figure in the area of the front door to the building.

"Get him!" the man said, barking out the command and pointing at the running Able Team commando.

Gadgets fired instantly.

There was no time to aim. He fired by instinct.

His partners were firmly convinced that he had at the very least a sixth sense and maybe seventh and eighth ones, as well. Even the cynical, hard-nosed Lyons—for whom the term *skeptical* was an understatement with regard to his thoughts on such matters as ESP and other parapsychological phenomena— recognized Gadgets's extraordinary abilities when it came to sensing things nobody else was aware of.

Gadgets fired three rounds from the hip with a single squeeze of the M-16's trigger. Three .223 projectiles, which Kissinger declared were not slugs, exploded into the man's head.

Nice job, he thought. I'll bet that made his face red.

The Able Team genius was always thinking on several different levels at the same time.

His ability to do so had never seemed particularly remarkable to him. It was just something that he had always done. As a kid, for instance, he had listened to music or watched TV while he studied—to no great detriment to his education.

His teachers had always warned him against that. "It's distracting," they'd said. "You simply can't give proper attention to two things at once." But Gadgets had soon learned the opposite was true; if he didn't occupy that part of his mind that liked music or TV while the rest of him studied, *then* he was distracted.

He once tried to explain this to one of his teachers, Miss Bird. At the time, Gadgets was in the ninth grade, and Miss Bird, a tall, angular, humorless woman in her forties, was his creative writing teacher.

She was not amused by his explanation.

"Don't be ridiculous, Hermann," she scolded. "You're only fooling yourself. You can't possibly be creative while you're listening to music."

Then, presumably as a means of encouraging his creativity, she decided he should write a hundred lines.

"Oh, Miss Bird—" the words came out in a loud, complaining groan "—don't make me do lines just because you don't agree with me. Jeez, man."

"Two hundred."

"Miss Bird!"

"Three?"

"Yes, ma'am. I mean, no, ma'am. I mean, whatever you want, Miss Bird."

She relented somewhat and settled on two hundred lines: "I will not listen to music while I study, because it is distracting."

What Miss Bird never knew was that Gadgets modified the text somewhat for the majority of the lines.

On the assumption that she would never do more than glance at the lines to see that the pages were filled, he composed a different resolution. He reasoned that as long as each line was approximately the same length and began and ended with the words she had specified, he could vary the text a little in the middle.

The results pleased him. After all, it *was* a creative writing class: "I will not stop looking up Sara's dress even though it is distracting."

"Sara" was Sara Yoder, who sat in the back of the class. She was dark and pretty and, more importantly to the young Schwarz—though he might not have put it this way—she was what was sometimes called an early bloomer.

Gadgets and several of the other boys in the front of the class thus found it convenient to frequently drop their pencils on the floor, so that when they bent down to pick them up, they could also take long lingering looks beneath the desk to the back of the row where Sara sat.

As finally submitted, the lines were impressive.

Two hundred lines at twenty-five per page came to eight pages. The first three sheets bore the original text composed by Miss Bird. The next four contained the R-rated version, and the last one was back to the original.

Miss Bird's lines taught the young Gadgets one valuable lesson: there are some ideas that are best kept to one's self.

The world just isn't ready for them.

Despite the best efforts of the well-intentioned Miss Birds of the world, Gadgets found that his ability to engage in critical thinking about several ideas at once didn't go away as he grew up. As a result, although he didn't ordinarily talk aloud to himself as the Bear did, using different sectors of his brain, he often did think of different things at the same time. And with his wisecrackcr personality, he sometimes found himself joking to himself in the middle of a firefight.

The man with the red face, his head no longer functional, slumped out of sight.

That threat out of the way, Gadgets's eyes probed the dusk for new enemies as he ran, seeking the men to whom the command, "Get him!" had been issued.

Seconds later, chest heaving, he pulled up behind the rusting car body. At that moment an exultant war whoop that could only be from Kissinger reached him. It came from somewhere beyond and behind the house, out of his sight.

Crazy bastard, Gadgets thought. But he still didn't sense anybody coming at him from the house.

A guttural grunt snapped into his consciousness. Even as he wheeled to face it, he knew he was in trouble.

Dogs!

In the fading light, the Able Team commando could make out two stocky shadows charging at him from the house. They didn't run with the powerful grace of a German shepherd or even a Doberman pinscher. No, these were shorter, huskier. They moved in a ponderous, powerful way, more like quarter horses than thoroughbreds.

White teeth and white foam around the slavering jaws riveted his gaze.

Pit bulls, he realized as he saw their tan shorthaired coats. They had been trained, too, and not to be watchdogs; they hadn't barked, but had merely attacked. Killing, not warning, was their bag. Even the grunt he had heard was involuntary, a sound from the effort of running, rather than any sort of warning.

For a split second, fear and adrenaline, usually the supreme motivators, paralyzed him.

Maybe it was something instinctive, a holdover of irrational terror from when man's ancestors were hunted by predators of years ago. Maybe it was the shock of expecting one kind of enemy and confronting another.

Whatever the reason, he froze momentarily. Then the paralysis left, and he was back in business.

"Die, fuckers!"

He crouched and pivoted from his hips as he yelled the war cry. The rushing forms were about eight feet away. Holding the M-16 in his right hand, he snapped off a single, quick shot.

It was all he got. No second chances.

Still, he reflected, the shot was a good one.

It hit squarely in the chest of the leading dog. His six or seven or eight senses perhaps heightened by the rush of adrenaline, Gadgets fancied he could almost see the streaking projectile part tan hair and flesh as it hit in dreadful slow motion. For the first time, the beast made a sound like a dog.

Even then, however, its killer instinct came through.

It wasn't a yelp or even a bark. Instead, a single deep snarl exploded from the pit bull's chest.

So great was the dog's momentum that the forward motion of the now-dead beast was not halted despite the pounds of force that had hit it in the chest. Its legs stopped working, and it stumbled and bounced on the weedy ground, but the dog's fifty-odd pounds of dead muscle slammed into Gadgets's legs even as the second pit bull made its final leap.

No time to shoot that one.

Gadgets threw up his left arm to deflect the attack and felt a vice with teeth on it clamp around his forearm, midway between elbow and wrist.

The heavy sleeve of his flak jacket saved his arm from a savage mauling. Still, the shielding material only blunted the points of the teeth as the dog ground his arm. A vicious snarling growl rumbled in the dog's throat.

Must be the rules against barking or making other noises are off once he gets a grip on a target, he thought facetiously.

Gadgets had taken a quick, involuntary step backward as he'd absorbed the impact of the dog's squatty body hitting him. Now he finally lost his balance and fell heavily on his back, the dog on top of him.

Being up close, face-to-face with the enraged beast was a nightmare.

Gadgets could see the muscles in the beast's jaws bulge as it worked to chew through his jacket and his arm, and he felt the dog's short huffs of fetid breath, hot and damp, against his face. A heavy, rotten-meat smell surrounded him. Claws like nails gripped and dug into the flesh of his body and legs. Crazily, when one scrabbling paw raked his groin, part of his mind quipped on how lucky he was that the beast's jaws weren't clamped around *that* area.

After all, he thought, it's about the same size as my forearm, isn't it?

Don't answer that, he said in his mind.

Back to the business at hand, he thought. Better stop with the mental wisecracks and get on with doing something about the dog. If I don't, I just might end up as Alpo for old Spot here.

He let go of the pistol grip on the M-16 and snatched a survival knife from its sheath.

Still on his back with the dog on top of him, Gadgets held the knife with the blade protruding from the thumb-and-forefinger side of his fist. He drove the knife in deeply, up to the hilt. It took a strong, powerful blow to do it. Once the knife was inside the dog's body, he twisted it and sliced downward, hoping the point and blade would find lung and heart.

A savage roar escaped from the dog's jaws, and the pressure on Gadgets's arm seemed to increase tenfold.

"Aaahhh!" he gasped as incredible pain surged through him. Oh, God, the fucker's going to rip my arm off, sleeve and all, he thought. It felt as if the flak jacket wasn't even there, though he knew his arm would have been shredded pork if it weren't.

Man and beast struggled in growling, mortal frenzy. Hot blood soaked Gadgets's right hand as he struggled to keep the blade rammed into the dog's muscular, spasming body. He gripped the grooved hilt for all he was worth, as the dog's thin, slippery blood threatened his hold. His mind wasn't wandering now. This was life and death.

Miss Bird would have been proud of him.

Another savage growling rose from the struggling forms. This time, however, it wasn't the pit bull. The growling came from Gadgets.

The Able Team commando had reverted to beast. Guttural snarls tore from his throat as he fought. With a powerful heave, he shoved off his back and rolled to one side, struggling to get on top of the flailing dog.

For a moment it was close.

The dying pit bull struggled in a renewed frenzy. Then superior weight prevailed, and Gadgets was on top of the beast, using his forearm to lever the dog's head back against the hard ground, pressing his weight down and mauling the dog's insides with the survival knife.

The pressure on his forearm weakened. Gadgets realized it was all but over, that all he had to do was hang on, and he concentrated on doing that and on listening for any signals of other enemies, either the two- or four-legged kind.

Then it was over, and Gadgets climbed off the still form and got to his feet. The whole thing had taken maybe thirty seconds or a minute.

Gadgets shook off the dread that the struggle with the dog had inspired. Even in death, the pit bull's lips still curled back from its cruel, yellowed teeth.

Gadgets had killed untold numbers of men in hand-to-hand combat. None had brought him to the level of sheer panic that the fifty pounds of now-dead dog meat had inspired in him. All in all, getting back to two-legged adversaries looked pretty good at the moment.

Wiping the slippery blood off on his trouser legs, he resheathed his knife and looked around for his M-16.

He found the gun and picked it up, scanning the house as he did so.

Nothing moved.

He was conscious of gunfire around the right side of the house, where Blancanales presumably was. It struck him that if the battle was concentrated there, this would be a good time to take the front of the house.

There was a sudden movement at his feet. It came from one of the dead dogs.

Gadgets leaped sideways and brought the M-16 to aim at the prostrate forms. Even as he realized that both dogs were indeed dead and that the movement had to be only the twitch of nerve fibres, he raked both shapes with gunfire.

He held the trigger down longer than was necessary. Then the terror subsided, and he relaxed slightly.

Animals that charged silently in the darkness are bad enough, he thought. Animals that you can't kill or that come back to life after you have killed them are a hundred times more frightening. Hell, a thousand times.

He had to do something to overcome his fears, use some psychological ploy to put things back in their proper perspective.

Stepping forward, he nudged one of the still forms with his toe. Then shaking his finger at the dead dog, he said, "Next time I tell you to fetch my slippers, you do it! You understand?"

The beast didn't respond.

"And no teeth marks in 'em, either. Teeth marks are bad news!" And how, he thought, wondering what his arm looked like under the flak jacket. It throbbed with a dull pain.

"And don't be crapping on the front lawn, either."

Turning his attention back to the house, he verified that it looked clear and sprinted toward it.

A figure moved in one of the window openings.

Gadgets fired from the hip; scratch another one. Then, as a matter of general principle he raked the front of the house as he rushed it.

The low porch lay before him. It was only some eighteen inches higher than the ground. He prepared to increase the length and height of his next stride.

A shallow, almost flat cardboard box that had once held a pizza lay on the ground before him. It was new, doubtlessly tossed there by the Aryan supremacists. Apparently tossing garbage out the front door of the house didn't detract from their firm conviction that the future of mankind lay in eliminating all who weren't like themselves.

"Dirt bags," he muttered.

Partly because it lay in his path and he was hauling ass and partly out of disgust for the enemy, Gadgets trod directly on the pizza box as he prepared to push off for the leap onto the porch.

A figure loomed again at one of the windows. He swung his rifle up and fired.

One round went off, and the weapon locked open, empty. And the one round, he knew, had missed its target. Better check the gun when this is over, he thought. It wasn't supposed to miss. Or run out of ammo, for that matter.

Way off to his left, at the left edge of the house, another man moved.

He was bracketed.

His only chance lay in continuing his charge to get next to the house, out of the field of fire, so he could reload.

He pushed off of the cardboard box even as the man in the window raised an automatic weapon and fired. The slick cardboard slipped along the weeds, and Gadgets's foot went out from under him. He fell heavily, clipping his head on the edge of the porch as he went down just as the blast of gunfire cut through the air where he would have been if he hadn't fallen.

The world swam, then seemed to recede. He didn't go completely out. Instead, he felt as if he was looking at everything through a long tunnel. Then a wave of blackness came over him, and he felt himself going down and out.

At that precise moment, Blancanales came around the house from the right.

## 16

The blast of the grenade from upstairs shook the old wood-frame house.

Startled, the man at the far end of the porch momentarily interrupted his firing to look up at the house, as if trying to see what was going on. Then, when he realized there was nothing to see from his vantage point anyway, he remembered his targets and swung back toward them.

He was too late.

Blancanales fired a controlled burst from the M-16. It caught the terrorist in the center of mass, the chest, and knocked him backward off the porch and onto the weed-choked ground beyond.

At the same time, the Politician heard the familiar voice of Kissinger from somewhere way to the rear of the house. It began as a war whoop, and ended as something else.

"Eeee-ya-*shit*!"

A hail of gunfire accompanied the oath. Something must not be going too well back there, Pol thought.

A movement in front of him caught his attention. With a start, Blancanales realized there was somebody in the window only a few feet down from where he stood. The Politician froze, holding his breath, hoping the man would look outside, but not really believing it would actually happen.

It did.

The man in the window leaned out momentarily, trying to get a glimpse of his attackers.

I've got something for you, amigo, thought the Politician. It's like the old good-news-and-bad-news line, and it's just for you, pal.

The bad news is that leaning out was a mistake.

The good news is that it's your last one.

A blast from the Politician's M-16, fired along the wall of the building, all but took the terrorist's head off. Sorry about your head, amigo, but here's something else for you. It's not quite the same, but it'll take your mind off your troubles, assuming I didn't take your mind off, period.

Blancanales moved up and lobbed a grenade through the window.

As he waited for the detonation, Pol gathered himself. This assault felt a lot like the games he and Kissinger had been playing at Stony Man Farm what seemed a million years ago. One thing was different, though—seriously different.

This time the guys inside, if there were any left, would be shooting back.

Of course, there might not be any left. But the only way to find out was to give them a target by going through the door.

He hated that idea.

Any hostiles inside would know the entry would be through one of three places, counting the windows. All they would have to do was step behind a wall or be in another room when the grenade went off, then step out and watch the likely spots.

I wonder what they pay ducks in a shooting gallery, the Politician thought. Whatever it is, it ain't enough. Unless they have a damn good union.

Of course, the grenade would help equalize things. Even if the hostiles managed to duck behind cover, chances were their ears would be ringing. There would be a lot of smoke in the room, which wouldn't help them, either. But they'd still know where to be looking, while he didn't even know the layout of the room and would be looking over an unfamiliar scene for a concealed enemy.

Where's Kissinger when I need him, the Politician wondered.

Not because he'd done a lot of building entries, but because he was the rookie, the FNG, as they used to say in Nam, the fucking new guy. The low man on the totem pole.

What are FNGs for, anyway, if not to send in on dangerous entries?

Just nut up and do it.

As he gathered himself for the rush, Blancanales reminded himself that he'd been lucky so far. Even his bad luck, like the sentry and the leg wound, hadn't been as bad as it very easily could have been. And lately, his luck had been good. He'd been saved from the guy in the upstairs window by the Cowboy.

Go for it!

When his luck was running hot, Blancanales believed in pressing it for all it was worth. The theory had originally come from Lyons, whose philosophy was that luck was not something you used up. You weren't just issued a finite quantity of it. Instead, it was like surfing a big wave; the harder you *tried* to ride it, balls to the wall, the farther you *could* ride it. Usually.

"The more you have, the more you get, in other words," Lyons had said one day.

"Like women," the Politician had quipped.

"Exactly. But at some point, no matter how good it's looking, things are going to collapse, turn to shit on you. And when they do, you go from feast to famine, and you have to start all over again."

"Like women," the Politician repeated.

"Yes," his partner had agreed. "But, until that point, press it to the max."

The explosion from inside shook the frame of the house.

Leg throbbing, Blancanales broke from his position of relative safety and dashed along the porch. He cast a quick glance at Gadgets—first things first, he thought grimly, praying his comrade was still alive.

He halted in front of the old and splintered door midway along the porch. Then, using his shoulder, he smashed the door open and went in low and fast.

A dingy room lay before him in the near darkness.

Blancanales landed on his belly and scrabbled forward. His eyes probed the darkness for any sign of hostiles and found none. Or, more accurately, he saw several, but each had already been won over by a lead and copper injection or by the deadly grenade blast. They'd been rehabilitated, so to speak.

Wood creaked off to his left.

The Politician rolled instantly and raked the area with gunfire. The creaking continued, then intensified and a chunk of the ceiling caved in with the popping of splintering wood and the gravelly crash of plaster.

Oh, well, if there had been somebody there, he'd be dead, he thought.

A flight of stairs led upward. Satisfied that things were under control on the first floor, Blancanales sprinted toward them.

He took the steps in iambic pentameter. Two at a time, one at a time, two at a time, one at a time. Each time the front leg, the one he was stepping up with, was his good one, he took two steps. Each time it was the wounded leg, he made do with one. Then he was at the landing, and it was "nut up and do it" time again.

Room by room, he checked the upstairs, pressing his luck hard, riding it for all it was worth.

All negative. Nothing moved. Nothing was alive.

The Politician's thoughts turned instantly to Gadgets. He turned and limped hurriedly down the stairs and outside.

His partner was nowhere to be seen.

That was good news. If he can move, he's alive, Blancanales thought. Still, how alive was the question.

"Over here."

The words came from behind him. Startled, the Politician wheeled around. Belatedly the Politician remembered that when Gadgets wanted to be, he could be invisible and soundless.

Gadgets was on the corner of the porch on the right side of the house, where Blancanales had been earlier. He was apparently checking the warehouse in the rear of the lot, where Kissinger was. As he turned to greet his friend, Gadgets's toe caught on a raised and splintered board on the floor of the porch.

"You okay, amigo? What happened?" the Politician inquired urgently. Blood streamed down the right side of Gadgets's face from a wound somewhere near his hairline.

"I tripped."

"No. Not that," said the Politician, gesturing vaguely to the board Gadgets had caught his toe on. Then he pointed to the porch area where Gadgets had gone down when the shooting started. "I mean, what happened out there?"

"I tripped."

The words didn't register for a moment. Did not compute, in other words. Then Blancanales's eyes narrowed as he considered his comrade's words.

"You . . . tripped?" he finally repeated, pausing between the two words, his brow furrowed.

"Yeah, I tripped."

"Oh. You tripped, then."

"Sort of."

Blancanales nodded his understanding. "I see." Then he added, "What happened to your head?"

"I bumped it."

"You bumped it."

An exasperated look spread over Gadgets's face. "Yes, for Pete's sake. I hit it on the edge of the porch when I fell. I'm okay, for cryin' out loud."

"Hey, amigo, that's cool. If you say you're okay, you're okay. I was just worried because—" a broad grin spread over the Politician's face "—those bumps on the head can be real serious. In Special Forces we had a special name for 'em."

Gadgets made a rueful shrug. He knew he was in for some kidding. "Oh, yeah? What?"

As the unofficial medic for Able Team, Blancanales saw a chance to play his role to the hilt. "Owies. That's macho talk for head bumps. Owies. Does 'im want me to take-um look at 'im's owie?"

Gadgets shook his head and grimaced but said nothing. Blancanales continued.

"*How* did you trip? I mean, did you trip on something, at least? Or did you . . . just trip?"

The Able Team genius turned his head and mumbled his reply. "Pizza box."

"A piece of box?"

"No, man," Gadgets said in exasperation. "Pizza box, not a piece of box. I stepped on a goddamn pizza box and it slipped out from under me and I fell and bumped my head."

The Politician stared at his friend. Then a broad grin spread over his features. "This is some heavy shit, all right. We're talking Purple Heart for sure."

"Yeah, yeah, yeah."

"It'll probably be in the papers. Ought to be, anyway."

Gadgets gestured toward the rear of the property, where Kissinger presumably was. "Shall we get on with it?"

Blancanales grinned. "Yes, let's. Watch your step, though. If there's one pizza box, we have to assume there may be more."

They made their approach in classic style.

Blancanales went first, angling out to the right as well as forward. Gadgets stayed behind, crouched by the corner of the house, ready to return fire in case the enemy had taken the Cowboy out. Then, when Blancanales got to cover, Gadgets moved up, going more to the left, however.

Leapfrogging, they moved up one at a time.

They could have saved themselves the trouble.

As they neared the barn, a match flared. At the same time, a familiar voice spoke.

"Nice approach, guys. Real cute. I probably couldn't have killed either of you more than two or three times." The match illuminated the grinning face of Cowboy Kissinger as he held the flame to the cigar in his mouth. Then he shook the match out, leaving them in near darkness.

"Yeah, I know," the Politician responded, for once not irritated by Kissinger's tone. "But my partner's been through some heavy combat and took a couple of bad hits, so we had to go slow."

Kissinger sensed that Blancanales was being less than serious and let it go. He produced a flashlight from somewhere in his gear and turned it on. Nothing happened. He muttered something and banged it against his leg a couple of times until it lit up.

"Nothing but the finest," he grunted. Then he turned to the others, his grin illuminated by the background reflection of the flashlight.

"Well, gentlemen," he announced, "mission accomplished. Our jungle warfare expert here did, in fact, see the tractor, and after our hard-pitched battle— Actually it was a pretty interesting little firefight. Brief, to be sure, but exciting while it lasted. Anyway, after all that—" he paused dramatically "—*we* now control it."

"Hot damn!" exclaimed Gadgets.

"Not exactly," continued the Cowboy. "You see—"

"The radio!" Blancanales interrupted urgently.

A tiny red light glowed on the radio clipped to Gadgets's belt. Somebody was trying to call them. It was a system they used in lieu of an audible signal when stealth was important.

However, the light was not without its drawbacks. For one thing, the wearer had to keep an eye on the damn thing, and when the radio was clipped to the belt, it was easy to miss. Moreover, under certain circumstances—such as nighttime stalkings—the sudden appearance of a tiny red dot could reveal the wearer's location in a decidedly inconvenient way. Still, on the whole, it was better than the loud crackle and rush of static that accompanied an audible signal.

"Lyons?" inquired Kissinger.

Gadgets nodded. "It's gotta be." He unclipped the radio and winked at the other two. "RAT Team to RAT One," he announced into the mike.

There was a long pause, then a familiar voice crackled in reply. The rhythmic chop-chop-chop of helicopter rotors could be heard in the background. "Lyons here. Gadgets, buddy, is that you?"

"Affirmative, RAT One."

"Uh, yeah. What's the situation there?"

"Code Four. All under control. Are you en route?"

"That's affirmative. ETA five to ten minutes. Should I expect any resistance?"

Kissinger nudged Gadgets. "Tell him not from the enemy. But we aren't too thrilled about it, and we might put up a little."

Gadgets grinned but ignored the suggestions. "Negative."

"Roger. Over and out."

Even as Gadgets switched off the radio, the three men could hear the distant roar of an approaching helicopter.

Something Kissinger had started to say bothered Blancanales. "So what have we got?" he inquired. "Is the rig here?"

Without replying, Kissinger turned and pointed the flashlight into the huge shed.

The first thing they saw were the three dead hostiles sprawled just inside the building. Kissinger had evidently had his hands full and had come out on top.

The Politician remembered the aborted war whoop and figured the now-dead hostiles must have been responsible for it. Then the light from Kissinger's flash glinted off shiny metal in the darkness. Blancanales's heart leaped.

And sank an instant later.

The light shone full on the tractor part of the rig.

There was no trailer, no tank of nuclear isotopes. The powerful cab and engine assembly sat in stubby isolation in the cavernous structure.

Apart from that, the building was empty.

## 17

Able Team and Kissinger gathered in the shed. The chopper that had brought Lyons waited, rotors idling, in the clearing in front of the house.

Things did not look good.

Nine enemy dead, of course—clever, counting Fido and Spot. But no tank of nuclear waste. And, even worse, no clue as to where the hot stuff was.

"So now what?" inquired Kissinger.

Lyons shook his head grimly. "According to the letter to the President, this is D day. They said three days from when the letter was sent, and this is day three." He sighed heavily. "I guess we tell the chief we lost 'em."

"Then what?"

"Hope for the best, I guess. They can start looking again. Comb the hills. Informants. Maybe find everybody who ever knew Gunther and put their nuts in a vise until they tell whatever they know. Hell, maybe aerial reconnaissance—a tank that big shouldn't be too hard to spot, at least not if they focus on reservoirs where they might be gonna dump the stuff."

"We don't know that for sure," Gadgets reminded him gently. "That's just my guess, remember."

Lyons acknowledged his partner's candor with a tilt of his head. "There's that," he agreed.

Blancanales spoke up. "Before we do that," he began pensively.

"Yeah?" rejoined Lyons.

"Let's take a quick look around this place."

"What for?"

The jungle warfare expert shrugged. "Who knows? We won't know until we see it." Seeing the skepticism on the faces of his comrades, he went on to explain.

"Look. In some ways, these guys have been real pros. But in other respects, they're goddamn amateurs."

"What do you mean?" demanded Lyons.

"Hell, one of 'em stuck his head out the damn window to see where I was. That's pretty bush league. Almost as bad as if the dude tripped over a pizza box or something," he said without looking at Gadgets, making a grim effort at humor to stave off their sense of failure.

"Go on."

"Well, there just *might* be something written down that will give us a clue as to what's up and where."

Lyons was skeptical. "What are you saying? That maybe they left a book of plays lying around, like the NFL? That's really reaching, amigo."

"Why?" responded Blancanales.

"Remember, their raid on the plant was damn sophisticated, according to the boss. It seems pretty far-fetched to think we'd find a written plan of the conspiracy lying around."

"Maybe. Maybe not. I'll agree that some parts have been all pro. But look at some of their help. Maggot and Mikey, for God's sake. They're animals. Thugs.

Sure, they're tough, but they are hardly experienced soldiers.''

The Ironman considered it. "Maybe," he said shrugging.

"Besides," continued Blancanales, "it doesn't have to be a plan of the conspiracy, anyway. Hell, one of the dipshits could have left an auto club map lying around with the directions on it because he was too drugged out to remember them. You never know."

"He's got a point, Ironman," suggested Gadgets.

Lyons clenched his fists until the veins on his forearms stood out in sharp relief against his skin in the glow of Kissinger's flashlight. He was clearly chafing for some action. The others knew the strain he must be under because of Margaret's disappearance. Moreover, though it hadn't been discussed in the few minutes since the chopper arrived, they could guess the results of the Ironman's grim mission to Mexico. It showed in his face.

"All right," Lyons said shortly. "Let's do it. Quick search. If we haven't got something in ten or fifteen, I'll get on the air with Brognola."

As they started for the house, Gadgets added, "And watch out for any of 'em that might be playing possum." He was about to add something about how a snake can strike even after it's dead but decided against it—too much like his episode with the dead pit bulls.

"And watch out for pizza boxes," Blancanales murmured in a voice that only Gadgets could hear.

"And for God's sake if anybody's still alive, save 'em so we can see if they know anything. Just don't let the Politician here get to 'em, or we'll never get the chance to ask them word one," Gadgets retorted, referring to the round Blancanales had put through the head of the target he had missed during the drill.

"*If* they'll talk," muttered Kissinger.

"They'll talk." The Ironman's jaw jutted dangerously beneath narrowed, glacial eyes. "This isn't police work, buddy. We don't have to advise 'em of their rights. They'll talk."

"Oh, yeah. I forgot."

"Believe me. They'll talk," he repeated. "If they're alive, they'll talk."

Lyons and Blancanales headed for the house. Gadgets began looking around the shed, picking up and examining any papers that looked promising among the scattered litter.

Kissinger, meanwhile, opened the door to the cab of the tractor and pulled himself inside.

Almost immediately, he struck gold. He struck it in a big way.

The gold came in the form of a map, exactly as the Politician had guessed. It wasn't an auto club map— Blancanales hadn't been *that* close—but he'd been close enough. Most importantly the map contained directions to a water distribution point just northwest of the city of New York.

The spot was marked with a crude star that had been drawn in ink and surrounded by a circle. Above the star, a small irregular blue bubble indicating a reservoir or lake of some kind was printed on the map. In the margin, a legend identified the marked spot in hand-printed letters. MWD Fac. 6.

Metropolitan Water District, Facility 6.

He didn't know for certain the letters stood for that, but it made sense. It fit. And the more he looked at it, the more certain he became.

"Jackpot!" he breathed. "Holy mother of sleeping sheep! We've got it!"

Kissinger searched the rest of the cab but found nothing of interest. He did find a couple of magazines that depicted the unclad female in several natural and unnatural poses, which might have piqued his interest at least slightly under other circumstances. Made him twitch a little, so to speak. But apart from those, he came up empty-handed.

The Cowboy swung out of the cab and dropped to the ground.

By the light of his flashlight, he double-checked his find. Then he took a deep breath, threw back his head and signalled the others.

"Eeee-yah-hooo!"

COLD FURY GRIPPED the Ironman as he surveyed the scene before him.

They lay on a rise overlooking Facility Six of the Municipal Water District for the City of New York. Below them were the enemy: Delbert Gunther and his Cajun angel. Behind them, a half-mile away, was the helicopter that had deposited them there.

A grim satisfaction mingled with the fury. This is it, he thought. The end of the line, D day, zero hour.

Somebody had a rendezvous with death, Lyons knew. Maybe several people did.

The only question was who.

From their vantage point, Facility Six resembled a sprawling, upside-down teardrop. The fat part of the drop, the reservoir, an irregular lake that vanished in the distance, was farthest from them. The pointed part was closest to where they now lay and was truncated by a high, narrow dam of stained concrete.

Lyons looked at the dam.

It was night, but the entire facility was lit up like daylight. The dam itself sloped steeply into a chasm on the side away from the lake. Lyons estimated the dam's dimensions to be maybe a couple of hundred feet from one edge of the chasm to the other, and close to a hundred feet thick.

Behind the dam lay water for a large part of New York City.

Downstream lay the scores of thousands who drank the water, cooked with it, bathed their children in it, washed the dishes with it.

Proud parents would gently sponge the soft tiny pink or brown or black bodies of infants with it before zipping them into snuggly sleepers for the night. Human beings from four to ninety-four would get up in the middle of the night and drink a glass of it. Children would shriek as they turned hoses on one another or filled their mouths with it, distending their cheeks so they could squirt their playmates and dash away.

Soon, by a cruel combination of man's technical genius and his intolerant evil, Gunther and his crew intended to poison this precious substance more completely than nature alone could ever have dreamed of doing.

The horrors of radiation sickness, delivered right to your door, thought Lyons.

Here, have a glass. Drink it and die, because your skin isn't the same color as mine. What kind of sociopathic assholes could Gunther and his crew be?

Lyons thought of a still, stiff form with tiny feet and no face on a makeshift gurney, and it suddenly seemed even more important to him to stop these guys.

MWD Facility Six was not an actual reservoir for storage of the main water supply. Instead, it was one of several distribution stations—essentially small holding areas where the water could be routed to various parts of the intricate web of water mains that fed specific areas of the city.

The holding area would be fed from above by aqueducts that connected to the main reservoirs.

It was ideal for the ARC's scheme. The Aryan Right Coalition had put much thought into the plan.

Inside the dam, he knew, would be computer-controlled valves. The amount of water let into each of the arteries could be controlled by the operator. Zero to max flow, all at the push of a button.

Lyons nodded grimly to himself.

Chalk up another to Gadgets, he thought. I'm damn glad he's a white hat.

All Gunther and his ARC playmates had to do to carry out their scheme of poisoning what they saw as the racially inferior areas of the city was to shunt all the water into the right mains, then release the nuclear waste right above the dam.

Within a matter of minutes, the torrent of water would be poisoned and en route to whatever segment of the city these crazies had targeted.

"Beautiful," he muttered. "Just fucking beautiful."

Using binoculars, he scanned the dam below them.

The huge tank truck was parked on a restricted-access area at the top of the dam. How they had managed to get there, Lyons could only guess. But then, these were the same guys who had managed to get into a nuclear waste facility in the first place. Besides, once inside and in control of the water station, the security worked to their advantage: if the alarm didn't sound, it was unlikely that they would be disturbed. The same precautions designed to keep people like themselves out would also serve to keep others out.

Then he saw the symbol on the tanker.

For a moment he had to laugh.

In a twisted, perverted way, Gunther had style. Or at least a set of nuts. A yellow triangular symbol for nuclear material was emblazoned on the tank truck. The guys had affixed a sign telling the world the tanker carried exactly what Lyons knew it carried.

The tanker was attached to a different tractor, of course; the one ARC had originally used was back at the sawmill outside Troy. Good thinking, Lyons realized. Gunther must have known to switch rigs to avoid detection.

Mustn't underestimate this guy, he reminded himself.

Besides the tanker, he counted two vans and eleven men, plus Gunther.

That meant three apiece, the Ironman calculated grimly. He knew which three he wanted. Dibs, as they used to say in high school. You're mine, fuckers.

Maggot.

Mikey.

And the one ultimately responsible for it all, big Delbert Gunther himself.

Let's hope it works out that way, Lyons thought, thinking of the small stiff shape under a dirty sheet on a dirty cart in a dirty, goddamn hole in the wall— Whoa, now. Steady, Ironman, or you'll get so caught up in vengeance, in doing it right, that you'll get your own ass shot off.

Finally, their reconnoitering done, the four men withdrew to compare notes.

"How's the leg?" Lyons asked Blancanales in a low voice.

The Politician grinned, though his face had a grayish tinge that betrayed the degree of pain he was in. "It's a long way from my heart, amigo. I'll make it."

"Can you move?"

"Yes."

For the next five minutes, the four men related what they had seen. Four sets of eyes were invariably superior to one, and by the time they were done, each man had a pretty detailed composite picture of the layout.

"So," said Kissinger at last, "you got a plan?"

Lyons nodded. "Yep."

"What is it?"

The Ironman looked at him coldly. "Kill 'em."

A thin smile played over Kissinger's lips. "Great. No objection, as they say. Any particular plan to do that?"

"Sure. Sneak up and attack 'em."

The Cowboy nodded approvingly. "Short and sweet," he observed. "Brevity is the soul of fucking wit, after all. Let's hope it works."

"Let's hope so."

## 18

Lyons moved silently forward in the darkness.

Gadgets and Kissinger were behind him, spread out far enough so that a single grenade or burst of gunfire couldn't take them all out together. Blancanales, despite his assurances that his leg would hold up, had been stationed on the roof of a low building twenty yards back. He lay there, rifle ready, sniper-style.

They wore dark outfits. At first glance, the clothing looked jet black. However, a closer examination would show it wasn't.

The material actually consisted of an irregular mixture of extremely dark brown and black. "Nightcamou," Kissinger had called it when the other men had questioned him.

"Sounds like bullshit to me," Lyons had observed.

The Cowboy, who had come up with the idea for the material himself, shrugged. "It's damn near as dark as all black, and it just might break up the shape a little more than any solid color."

"Not too likely it'll ever make the difference between success and failure," persisted Lyons.

"Agreed," said the Cowboy. "But it *could*, and why not increase the odds in our favor, even if only by a little? Hell, Lyons, you can wear your bathing suit or your cop monkey suit if you want. But just don't stand too close to me."

Lyons had relented.

And, as they approached the dam, he had to admit that, whether the camouflage worked or not, the outfits felt damn good. The fabric was soft and silent. Both the pants and the long-sleeve jerseys were made of it.

The remainder of their outfits were basic black.

Black shoes. Black socks. Thin knit gloves, also black. And soft helmets that resembled ski masks made of the same mottled dark-brown-and-black fabric.

"Where are our raid jackets?" Kissinger whispered.

"What raid jackets?" inquired Blancanales.

"The RAT team vests, of course."

"Oh, yeah. Right. Well, I guess we'll just have to do this caper without 'em."

Each man carried identical weaponry. Again, Kissinger's influence had made it that way.

"It's fucking ridiculous, each guy carrying his own pet toys," he had announced a few months ago with characteristic Cowboy tact. "Everybody ought to have the same thing."

"I like my goddamn Python," argued Lyons, his jaw jutting.

The cop in him refused to die; even in this age of automatic pistols, he felt most comfortable with a .357 magnum revolver, either the Colt Python or the Smith & Wesson model 19 or 66. "I'll shoot rings around you with it," he added.

"Yeah. And Gadgets likes his rattler and the Politician here—hell, lover boy that he is, he probably uses a garter snake. And that means nobody is halfway good with anybody else's weapon. So if your gun takes a dive on you, you can't just pick up another guy's.''

"How often has that happened?'' demanded the Ironman.

"It *could* happen. And besides, if you run out of ammo, the other guy can't give you any unless the weapons are all the same. Christ, we're specialists, for Pete's sake, not some bunch of hillbilly irregulars.''

Even Lyons had to agree with the logic. Hard to argue with, he admitted.

Thus, on this occasion, it had been back to basics, the weaponry selected by the Cowboy.

"Your basic M-16, in attractive mat finish,'' Kissinger had said as he handed them out. "Your basic Colt Government Model in .45 ACP, with certain skillful modifications, courtesy of yours truly.''

Now one at a time, the three dark shadows slipped through the night toward a pile of concrete rubble some thirty yards to the near side of the dam. They made it unobserved, and grouped to survey the dam before them.

Spotlights mounted on tall poles ran along either side of the top of the thick concrete wall, and in rows at regular intervals along it. The lights lit up the surface like some futuristic parking lot.

About midway along the span, on the left side as Able Team looked at it, sat the huge tanker. Three men were working on something attached to the side of it. Others stood guard.

"What the hell are they doing to it?'' muttered the Cowboy.

"Explosives, I'd say,'' whispered Gadgets. "Some sort of shape charge, probably.''

Realization dawned on Kissinger. "Their can opener," he breathed. "They're going to blast the fucker open. Jesus, these guys are really gonna do it."

Gadgets nodded absently. "Probably going to drive the rig right over the side. When it's under water, they'll hit the button and presto! All that hot nuke stuff goes into the water supply."

"And a guy inside the dam at the controls..." continued Kissinger.

"You got it. Nuclear water, not $H_2O$, delivered right to your door."

The expanse of concrete on the top of the dam presented a hell of a problem.

It was flat and well lighted, making concealment impossible. Forty yards or so of wide-open space, with no greater cover than the light poles that ran across in rows. They were the old-fashioned, concrete variety and, as such, would certainly stop the 9 mm stuff the ARC seemed so fond of. But they weren't big enough around to provide complete protection, and they were damn few and far between.

"What we need," mused Lyons, "is some sort of vehicle."

"An armored personnel carrier," agreed the Cowboy. "Don't happen to have any spare APCs lying around, do you?"

Gadgets's response startled them.

"Yes," he whispered. "By God, yes, I think we do!"

Kissinger's brow furrowed. "What the hell you talking about?" he said. "There ain't gonna be any..." Then his gaze followed Gadgets's, and he paused in midsentence.

Slowly, a grin appeared on his face. It started small, then broadened and grew as realization dawned on him.

"Think so?" he breathed softly. "Do you really think so?"

"Why not?"

Lyons followed Gadgets's gaze and nodded slowly. "Why not, indeed? Why fucking A not?"

## 19

The Cat was yellow, and it was old.

Big son of a bitch, too, thought Lyons.

The Caterpillar D-8 bulldozer squatted ponderously some forty yards on their side of the dam. It was in a small clearing where apparently some grading was underway. From the looks of it, the folks who ran the dam wanted to build a storage yard of some kind and were rearranging the landscape with the dozer as part of the project.

"Our APC!" whispered Kissinger.

Gadgets nodded. "No way they'll shoot through that blade. Hell, it'd take armor piercing to even make a dent in it. That 9 mm stuff these guy's are using won't faze it."

"Do you know how to work one?" Lyons asked. "Can you start it even?"

"If it's operational and not broken down or something, I can start it."

Moments later they gathered next to the big Cat. Delbert Gunther and his nuclear henchmen were still busy at the middle of the dam, some sixty yards away.

"This is an old one," Gadgets whispered as they examined the Caterpillar.

Jesus, thought Lyons, this is one massive brute of a bastard. The Cat stood higher than his head. The tracks—heavy steel treads on each side, like those on a tank—stood some three or four feet high.

"How can you tell it's so old?" he asked.

Gadgets pointed to the blade and to a large drum behind the seat. "It's cable rigged," he explained, as though that answered the question.

"Thanks a hell of a lot. What's that mean?"

"A cable-rigged dozer has a blade that's lifted by a cable connected to a drum. The newer ones use hydraulics, pistons on arms—that sort of thing."

"Oh." Lyons looked at the big machine. "Think it works?"

Gadgets nodded. "I'd bet on it. Somebody has given this baby a lot of TLC—tender loving care. She's old, but she looks like she's in prime condition."

"There's one problem, though," Gadgets whispered.

Lyons's heart sank. "What's that?"

"You don't just climb on one of these babies and turn a key, then tool off to the store."

"What do you mean?"

"They're louder'n shit when you start 'em. And you gotta let them idle a minute or so before you take off, or the damn things are likely to die on you." He gestured at the motor. "Hell, this old bastard has a pony engine on it. You gotta start that little gas engine first. Then that engine turns over the main diesel until it starts."

"Shit." Lyons considered the problem.

Suddenly the whine and rumble of some other piece of heavy equipment starting up reached them.

They all pivoted to look toward the dam.

A huge crane had been fired up. Even at a distance, it made an incredible racket. As they watched, the crane started to move toward the tank truck.

"Looks like they weren't going to just drive the tanker over the edge after all," observed Gadgets. "Must be gonna lower it into the water with the crane."

Then, suddenly, he hauled himself into the Caterpillar.

Seconds later, a small gasoline engine coughed, then caught. When it was running smoothly, Gadgets engaged a clutch and the harsh metallic clatter of the diesel turning over reached their ears.

With a roar, the diesel caught. Heavy black smoke belched from the exhaust.

"Jackpot!" exclaimed the Cowboy excitedly.

The crane maintained its roll across the dam toward the tanker of hot stuff.

"Is this thing ready?" asked Lyons urgently.

Gadgets nodded. "If it ain't, it's just gonna have to lump it. Hop on, guys. Next stop, Armageddon!"

They clambered onto the massive piece of equipment. Gadgets was in the operator's seat, and Lyons and Kissinger crouched over and around him.

"Where's the steering wheel?" demanded Kissinger.

"Doesn't have one. Each track is separately powered. You control it by these clutches here." Gadgets pointed to a pair of levers in front of him. "To turn it, you disengage one clutch, which stops that side. The other side keeps on, pushing the damn thing around the one that's stopped."

"Let's haul ass!" hissed Lyons urgently.

"Ten four." Metal squealed and creaked as the cable-rigged blade came up off the ground. Gadgets lifted it until the half-inch-thick steel plate made a perfect shield in front of them. "Just like the Seabees did in the South Pacific," he said, grinning. Then he shoved the clutches forward, and they lurched into motion.

They hauled ass at about seven miles per hour. The noise was deafening, the ride as rough as rocks as the metallic tracks clawed forward, first along the rough ground that separated them from the dam and then, suddenly, along the dam surface itself.

Nobody saw them.

Even Gunther's would-be guards were looking at the huge crane, which by now had maneuvered itself next to the nuclear tank.

The D-8 Cat rumbled and clattered on, Gadgets at the controls, Lyons and Kissinger clinging to either side of his seat, their M-16s in hand.

"Come on, baby, go!" breathed Kissinger.

Gadgets checked the throttle. "Wide open. This is it, guys."

The gap closed. Still none of the hostiles noticed.

They were maybe forty yards from the enemy when suddenly the crane operator swiveled in his seat.

The other hostiles followed his gaze, then scrambled for their weapons.

"We're burned!" shouted Gadgets. "Here's where it gets lively, gents! Just don't let 'em get around to the side, and the blade will stop anything they've got!"

The men by the nuclear tanker scrambled and came up with their weapons. Orange flames and the hammering of 9 mm autofire met them.

An insistent clanging began as the slugs struck the massive steel blade. Instinctively the three men ducked, though they were already well protected by the blade.

Suddenly, Kissinger stood up. Gripping the operator's cage with one hand, he clamped the M-16 against his side with the other. His war whoop split the air.

"Eeeee-yaahhh—hoooo!"

The M-16 began to hammer out its response.

Puffs of cement dust rose as the projectiles struck the concrete surface of the dam. Ricochets screamed off into the distance. Then he found his range somehow, despite the bucking of the Caterpillar.

Men started dying.

Three men with automatic weapons jerked spasmodically as the hot .223 rounds smacked wetly into their bodies.

"Eeee-yaaahh-hoooo!"

Lyons, meanwhile, concentrated on the crane operator.

It took Lyons half a clip to do it, but then he found him. Some of the bullets glanced sparks off the steel of the crane, but others struck home. The crane operator's body jerked and twitched, then slumped over the controls.

The Ironman turned back to the tank truck itself.

A lone figure broke from the tanker and sprinted toward one of the vans. The man was squatty. Toad-like. Gray hair hung down from a balding head. Greasy biker's colors adorned the back of his leather jacket.

A second figure ran behind him, taller, less well coordinated.

Maggot and Mikey!

Lyons turned the rest of the clip at the targets. And all of another, even though the figures weren't running anymore.

One score settled.

Then they were there; the massive old Cat was clattering up on the enemy.

Braced on top of the tractor, Kissinger was cursing and firing on autoburn. Suddenly, his M-16 locked open, out of ammo. Three of the enemy, probably guys who had some military training and recognized the distinctive clack of an empty rifle, popped out from behind the crane, automatic weapons in hand.

Lyons swung to cover his partner while he reloaded. Lyons pulled the trigger to auto-burn the triple threat, but his weapon, too, locked open.

Empty!

"Shit!"

His fingers scrambled for a fresh clip, his body braced all the time for the hail of hot lead he expected would come at any moment from the three hostiles.

It started, all right, and then stopped as suddenly as it had begun.

A hail of hot projectiles struck the crane, near where the three men were. Ricochets sparked and whined. A bullet fragment hit Lyons on the jaw and blood flowed.

The three hostiles staggered backward as bullets tore into their bodies.

Lyons glanced quickly at Kissinger. The Cowboy was still reloading. Then he realized where the covering fire had come from.

"Blancanales! All right, amigo!"

The Ironman knew without looking farther that from his vantage point on the building, the former

Green Beret was auto-burning the three men. He would be prone, Lyons knew, and rock steady, dead on target.

Then he and Kissinger were reloaded, and it was time to clean up.

Moments later, there was nobody but Stony Man personnel left alive on the top of the dam.

Lyons let out a long sigh of relief. Glancing at his partners, he saw that everybody looked okay.

Nothing else moved.

And the blood, Christ, the blood! It was everywhere. It pooled around the bodies, then ran downhill on the gray cement, making long red fingers.

When I go to hell, thought Lyons crazily, they'll give me a paintbrush and a bucket of blood and I'll be painting the walls for eternity. Like the window washers on some of those huge skyscrapers. They never finish. By the time they've done the whole thing, they're back to where they began because all the windows need cleaning again.

That'll be my punishment. Like Sisyphus pushing his boulder, I'll be painting with warm blood forever.

I'm sorry, Margaret.

A sudden diesel roar startled them. It came from the tractor rig of the tank truck.

Lyons spun and looked up.

The first thing he saw was the black smoke from the exhaust pipe of the tractor. Then he saw the figure in the cab.

Gunther!

With a metallic crunch of gears, the tractor lurched forward. He was going to drive the tanker off the edge of the dam as Gadgets had originally theorized!

Lyons sprinted alongside the big rig. With a leap, he caught a handhold and hauled himself up on the driver's side.

The window was open. Gunther's huge form sat behind the wheel. He was urging the massive equipment toward the edge of the dam.

A white heat burned inside Lyons.

He thought of tiny feet and of a face torn off, of a body lying under a dirty sheet in a Mexican morgue. He thought of the dead guards at the nuclear waste site in Louisiana, whom he didn't know but had read about in the reports delivered to Brognola. He thought about the thousands of men, women and children downstream from where they now fought, people who didn't know he existed and would never know if he died.

Most of all, he thought of Margaret.

The Ironman levered himself up on the big mirror in front of the driver's door. Then, cocking his right arm, he drove a short, straight punch at Gunther's face.

Blancanales could call his shots when he was shooting firearms. Kissinger could do the same, though not quite as well. Lyons didn't pretend to be that kind of marksman, but he still knew what calling your shots was all about. Sometimes a man just knew that a given shot was a good one, dead center, ten ring. It had that feel to it.

Lyons's hard, straight-ahead right was like that. It had that feel to it.

Nose cartilage crunched and broke beneath his fist. Gunther's head snapped back, and he went suddenly rigid. As he did so, his foot came off the accelerator. The sudden deceleration almost hurled Lyons from his perch, but the truck slowed to barely more than a crawl. Then Lyons leaned in and killed the engine, and the big rig lurched to a stop.

Suddenly the truck door slammed open, and Gunther surged out. Lyons tried to keep his grip, couldn't, and dropped backward to the cement surface of the dam.

Gunther jumped down after him.

Lyons came up out of a crouch and threw three quick blows into the man's massive body. They were good shots, each packing all the force of the Ironman's legs, hips, body and arms.

Gunther staggered backward against the tractor. Then, surprisingly, he ducked and rolled under the rig.

"The detonator!" Gadgets shouted the warning as Gunther emerged from under the trailer and moved toward the jerry-rigged apparatus on the side of the cylinder. It was the same piece of equipment they had seen Gunther's men working on earlier from across the dam.

The huge man tore at a metal box.

A cover came off, and Lyons could see a timer of some sort. Then, in terrible slow motion, they saw Gunther twist the timing mechanism out and hurl it to the ground, then stab for a button inside the metal chassis....

The three Stony Man warriors scrabbled backward, then turned and sprinted away, would-be Olympians in a hundred-meter race.

Behind them, the device detonated.

Fragments of steel blasted into the Aryan leader's body. The explosion cut a rent in the side of the steel tank, releasing a stream of radiation that followed the shrapnel.

The Cajun angel had claimed her first victim.

Her creator.

# EPILOGUE

From the *Los Angeles Times*:

New York. A tank truck leaking deadly chlorine gas was discovered at a water reservoir outside New York City last week it was learned yesterday.

In a prepared statement, Richard Whited, director of the Department of Public Health, told reporters that the truck was found on top of the dam at Facility Six of the Metropolitan Water District. The facility is a distribution point where water from other reservoirs is held and then routed to various areas of the city.

Whited stated the gas, which is toxic in its purest form, is used to maintain water quality. The tank had apparently developed a leak along a seam on one side, and a small quantity of the gas escaped. However, according to officials, the incident posed no threat to public health.

Carl Lyons had reread the article, then tossed the newspaper aside before he had left for the church.

His thoughts returned to it now that the ceremony was over. For the better part of a week, no news whatsoever concerning the incident had appeared.

Then, finally, this innocuous article had shown up on page seventeen of the *Times*.

Somebody had done a hell of a job to squelch that.

Hell, if the antinuke idiots had gotten hold of the real story, it would have been headlines, page one.

Then another thought struck him. What if the cover-up itself became known? Hell, if the well-to-do liberals who opposed nuclear power got hold of the real story, it would be a replay of Watergate.

What the hell, he thought. All in a day's work. Another day, another dollar.

Lyons loosened his tie and started to unbutton his collar, but his white pallbearer's gloves got in the way. He peeled them off and stuffed them into the pocket of his suit as he walked toward his rental car. A handful of mourners straggled behind him, moving away from the grave, away from the dead and back toward their jobs and their lives.

Today and tomorrow and every day after that, new products would be released on the market. New housing developments would be built, boys and girls would fall in love as others fell out of it.

It was all part of life, though Margaret wouldn't see any of it.

But he knew—he believed—that in one sense she was still alive. Who was it that said you're not dead until the last person with fond memories of you is dead, too, he asked himself.

Lyons took out the white gloves and dropped them into a trash container near his car. They were for carrying the dead, and he'd done that. Now he wanted to carry the part of her that was still alive, the fond memories.

In the final analysis, they hadn't quite been able to love each other, at least not completely. How was it she had put it? We're close, but we just don't fit somehow?

But the fond memories were there nonetheless. And as long as he lived, part of her would, too.

That was okay.

Pretty good, in fact.

Good enough, anyway.

A damn sight better than painting the walls of hell with a bucket of blood for the rest of eternity.

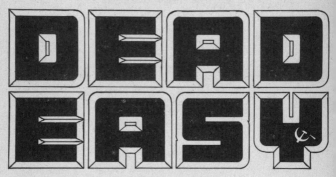

# DON PENDLETON'S EXECUTIONER

# MACK BOLAN™

Baptized in the fire and blood of Vietnam, Mack Bolan has become America's supreme hero. Fiercely patriotic and compassionate, he's a man with a high moral code whose sense of right and wrong sometimes violates society's rules. In adventures filled with heart-stopping action, Bolan has thrilled readers around the world. Experience the high-voltage charge as Bolan rallies to the call of his own conscience in daring exploits that place him in peril with virtually every heartbeat.

"Anyone who stands against the civilized forces of truth and justice will sooner or later have to face the piercing blue eyes and cold Beretta steel of Mack Bolan...civilization's avenging angel."
— *San Francisco Examiner*

**GOLD EAGLE**

Available wherever paperbacks are sold.

MB-2R

# Mack Bolan's

# PHOENIX FORCE

## by Gar Wilson

The battle-hardened, five-man commando unit known as Phoenix Force continues its onslaught against the hard realities of global terrorism in an endless crusade for freedom, justice and the rights of the individual. Schooled in guerrilla warfare, equipped with the latest in lethal weapons, Phoenix Force's adventures have made them a legend in their own time. Phoenix Force is the free world's foreign legion!

**"Gar Wilson is excellent! Raw action attacks the reader on every page."**

**—Don Pendleton**

Phoenix Force titles are available wherever paperbacks are sold.

PF-1

# TAKE 'EM NOW

## FOLDING SUNGLASSES FROM GOLD EAGLE

Mean up your act with these tough, street-smart shades. Practical, too, because they fold 3 times into a handy, zip-up polyurethane pouch that fits neatly into your pocket. Rugged metal frame. Scratch-resistant acrylic lenses. Best of all, they can be yours for only $6.99. **MAIL ORDER TODAY.**

Send your name, address, and zip code, along with a check or money order for just $6.99 + .75¢ for postage and handling (for a total of $7.74) payable to Gold Eagle Reader Service, a division of Worldwide Library. New York and Arizona residents please add applicable sales tax.

Remove from pouch...

unfold once...

unfold twice...

and they're ready to wear.

**GOLD EAGLE**

Gold Eagle Reader Service
901 Fuhrmann Blvd.
P.O. Box 1325
Buffalo, N.Y. 14240-1325

GES1-RRR

*Offer not available in Canada.*